BOOKS BY DEAN HUGHES

Nutty for President
Honestly, Myron
Switching Tracks
Millie Willenheimer and the Chestnut Corporation
Nutty and the Case of the Mastermind Thief
Nutty and the Case of the Ski-Slope Spy
Jelly's Circus
Nutty Can't Miss
Theo Zephyr
Nutty Knows All
Family Pose
Nutty, the Movie Star
Nutty's Ghost

Nutty's Ghost

by Dean Hughes

Atheneum   1993   New York

Maxwell Macmillan Canada
Toronto

Atheneum
Macmillan Publishing Company
866 Third Avenue
New York, NY 10022

Maxwell Macmillan Canada, Inc.
1200 Eglinton Avenue East
Suite 200
Don Mills, Ontario M3C 3N1

Macmillan Publishing Company is part of the Maxwell Communication
Group of Companies.

First edition
Printed in the United States of America
10 9 8 7 6 5 4 3 2 1
The text of this book is set in 12 point Garamond.
Book design by Tania Garcia

Library of Congress Cataloging-in-Publication Data

Hughes, Dean. 1943–
Nutty's ghost / by Dean Hughes. —1st ed.
p.   cm.
Summary: Eleven-year-old Nutty isn't sure he wants to be an actor
when he has to contend with an overzealous director, jealous
friends, and a strange apparition that doesn't want the movie he is
starring in to be made.
ISBN 0–689–31743–3
[1. Ghosts—Fiction. 2. Motion pictures—Production and
direction—Fiction. 3. Actors and actresses—Fiction.] I. Title.
PZ7.H87312Nx 1993
[Fic]—dc20   92–8530

For Brad and Amy Russel

Chapter 1

*N*utty felt like a sleepwalker. It was six
o'clock in the morning and he was dead
tired, but he had to go get his makeup on.
That's not to say that Nutty had started wearing
makeup—not normally—but he was a star now.
A movie star. For two weeks he had been shooting
a film, which was set right in his hometown of
Warrensburg, Missouri, and Nutty was playing the
leading part. Right now he was on his way to the
set, just a few blocks from his house.

The truth was, Nutty was not so excited about
show business as he had thought he was going to
be. He and his friend William Bilks had worked
hard to get Nutty's first movie role. The whole
thing—the role *and* the movie—had turned out
to be stupid, and now this new one was looking
just as bad. And stardom was greatly overrated, as

far as Nutty was concerned—especially when it meant getting up this early in the morning.

Nutty turned a corner, around a hedge, but he had his eyes only half open. He almost ran into a guy who was standing in the middle of the sidewalk. Nutty came to a sudden stop and looked at the man. What he saw was *very* strange. The man was older, and he wore his graying hair long, almost to his shoulders.

But that was not the strangest part.

The guy was dressed in some sort of weird outfit—like an old Spanish explorer, or . . . Nutty didn't know what. He had on a fancy green vest and a silk shirt, and those puffy little trousers that are only about as long as shorts. And below that, long green stockings.

"Are you Parker House?" the man said, and he made a deep bow, swinging his arm across himself. His voice was *grand*—deep and British.

"Yeah," Nutty said, but he was surprised the man would know his name—especially his "stage name."

"Just as I thought. I have a message for you."

Nutty nodded and waited, the whole time checking this guy out. He wasn't someone from the movie company—at least not anyone Nutty had seen before.

"There's been an alteration of plans this morning," the man said. "The film location has been changed. I am to tell you that you should appear at the Springs known as Pertle rather than at the laboratory school—as previously scheduled."

"Clear out at Pertle Springs?"

"Yes, sir. That is correct."

"Then why didn't they pick me up? They always send a car if I have to go very far."

"Sir, I cannot answer that." He bowed again, as if to apologize. "I can only deliver the message that was given me."

Nutty was disgusted. Who had sent this weird guy, anyway? And why had the director changed the shooting location? It didn't make sense. Nutty would have to go back home and get a ride to Pertle Springs, which was out on the edge of town.

"Okay. Well . . . thanks," Nutty said, and the man dropped into another low bow. Nutty wanted to tell him to lay off the act. Instead, he said, "Who are you, anyway?"

"Matthew Graham at your service, sir."

That explained nothing at all. Still, Nutty could think of nothing better to do than to thank the man again, and then he turned around and headed home. As he turned the corner, he glanced back to catch a last look at Mr. Graham.

But he was gone!

Nutty stopped and looked around. The guy

hadn't crossed the street, and there was nowhere else to go, except into one of the houses. And yet, Nutty knew the names of all the people who lived in the houses on that street, and Graham wasn't one of them. Nutty had never seen this man in Warrensburg before.

It was very strange. Nutty had no idea what to make of the whole situation, but he figured he better get to Pertle before Mr. Deveraux, the director, threw one of his tantrums. So Nutty hurried home and woke up his parents.

Nutty's dad agreed to drive Nutty to the new location, but he took his sweet time, as far as Nutty was concerned. He said he would take "just a quick shower"—and grab a cup of coffee—and then go straight to work after he dropped Nutty off. But it was almost forty-five minutes before he and Nutty were on the road. Nutty was almost an hour late when he reached Pertle.

"Son," Mr. Nutsell told Nutty, "if they're going to change locations on you at the last minute, and not send a driver, then they have to accept the fact that you're going to be late. You're not an extra in this film, remember; you're the *star*. And that means something. If you don't act like a star, they won't treat you like one. That's a very important lesson to learn in this life."

Dad was tall and blond—like Nutty. And he had a freckle-faced innocent look about him—also like Nutty. When he tried to sound important, he sounded to Nutty like a kid trying to act grown up.

Nutty did a lot of nodding and ignoring. He was trying to spot the movie company. What he saw made no sense at all. There were no big trucks parked near the lake, no people. A whole movie company wasn't that hard to spot. What was going on?

Dad drove around the lake, and around the whole area, and by now he was really fuming. "I say that you go home and wait for them to come looking for you. Nothing happens until they get you to the set. They know that."

That was true, but Nutty knew what a pain in the old you-know-what Mr. Deveraux could be. "Okay, just take me back home," Nutty said. "But drive past the lab school on the way. That's where we were shooting yesterday, and that's where they *said* we'd be today."

It was summer now, but during the school year Nutty attended a laboratory school at the university, not far from his house. That's where much of the film was being shot.

As Mr. Nutsell drove up to the school, Nutty could see the film crew. The trucks and trailers were all parked where they had been the day before. Nothing had moved.

"Oh, for crying out loud, Nutty," Mr. Nutsell

said, "someone misled you entirely. What's going on?"

Nutty didn't take the time to answer. He jumped out of the car and hurried up to the set. He expected to get chewed out. But things actually seemed on hold. People were standing around, apparently waiting out some sort of delay.

Still, William Bilks came striding out to meet Nutty, and he looked concerned. "Well, I'm glad you came back. We won't start the shoot over for a while, but you gave me a scare when you took off like that."

William sounded stern. He stopped and began shuffling his feet—like Nutty's grandpa. William was only eleven, but he was a genius—a genuine child prodigy. He went to a private school and at night took college classes, but none of that was challenging enough for him. He spent most of his time reading or doing his own scientific experiments.

"I don't think the actor is hurt all that seriously," William continued, "but he needed a little rest."

"William, what in the heck are you talking about?"

"The actor you hit, of course."

"Hit? I didn't hit anyone. When? Yesterday?"

William rolled his eyes. He was wearing his

little gray sweater, all buttoned up, even though the June morning was humid and the day was going to be very hot. "Nutty, don't do this. I don't have the patience for it this morning. I think you're starting to think you're a star and you can—"

"William, I don't know what you're talking about. I didn't hit *anyone*."

William stared at Nutty. Finally he said, "If you're trying to fake amnesia, it isn't going to work. And there's no use denying it anyway. No one thinks you meant to hit the guy. You're not in trouble for that. You're only in trouble for wandering off."

"Stop a minute," Nutty said. "This is crazy. I'm not *back*. I just got here. And I haven't been wandering. I've been trying to find the set. I got a message that we were moving out to Pertle, so I've been out there."

Now the boys were both staring. Nutty was completely confused, and he could see that William was just as mixed up himself.

"Are you telling me you haven't been here this morning?" William asked.

"Sure I am. Are you telling me that I have been?"

"Nutty, don't you remember the fight scene we shot?"

"I told you, I wasn't here."

Now William was really getting big eyes. "Nutty, you were acting out a fight scene, and you were supposed to swing and miss the fellow, but you clubbed him in the jaw. You don't remember that?"

"No way."

William seemed to believe Nutty. He considered for a time before he said, "Maybe you were also struck, and now you're—"

"William, my dad and I have been driving around trying to find the stupid set. Ask *him* if you don't believe me."

"But I saw you. You talked to me. You played your part."

The boys were back to staring at each other.

Just then Sarah Montag—the film's "leading lady"—walked up to them. She was dressed in a calico dress and had her hair in pigtails (Mr. Deveraux's idea of what a country girl should look like). It was the same costume as the day before.

"Nutty, why did you take off? No one thought you did it on purpose."

Oh, wow. This was getting spooky.

"Sarah," William said, "Nutty doesn't remember being here this morning."

"It's not that I don't remember," Nutty said. "I wasn't here. I told you where I was."

William nodded, and Nutty saw a certain look

come into his eyes. It was the look he got when he was processing information, reaching conclusions, working out new theories. He turned to Sarah. "Did you notice anything strange about Nutty this morning?" he asked.

"No . . . not exactly."

"But you did notice something. What was it?"

"Well, it's just that his acting seemed better than usual. Mr. Deveraux hardly had to yell at him."

"Yes. I noticed the same thing."

"Anything else?"

"No . . . not really."

"Come on. What else?"

"Well, his eyes looked sort of different. I thought maybe he was tired."

"Interesting that you noticed that. I saw it too. A strange sort of translucence. I wondered about it at the time."

"William," Nutty said, "I've told you about ninety times now—I wasn't here."

"Exactly. I think you weren't."

But now it was Sarah who was surprised. "William, you know he was here."

"No, I don't. Nutty, who gave you the message about changing locations this morning?"

Nutty told his story.

William was fascinated with every word. When

Nutty finished, William said, "Just as I thought. I've had a suspicion of something like this ever since we started shooting. Think how many things have gone wrong. We've had one disaster after another, every day."

"Yeah, well, this movie crew *stinks*," Sarah said.

"That's how it seems to us," William said. "But the crew claims they have never seen so many strange things happen. We've had sets fall over, cameras go haywire—even people trip when nothing appeared to be in the way."

Nutty had to admit that some of the things that had happened did seem more than just strange. One day an actor had suddenly fallen over backward, as though he had been pushed, but no one had touched him. Another time, after shooting a scene, nothing had shown up on the film—and yet the camera had been rolling the whole time.

"Something else strikes me as really very extraordinary," William said, and Nutty could see that William was getting excited now. He was talking fast, looking happy. "The actor you hit this morning—or so we all thought—was a huge fellow. And yet, you knocked him flat. I was amazed to think you could hit anyone that hard."

Nutty was not just worried anymore; he was scared. "It wasn't me, William. I'm not lying. It *wasn't* me."

10

"But you don't have a twin," Sarah said.

It was William who answered. "True. But he may have a ghost."

"What?" Nutty said, and this time he was pretty sure that William had come up with his wildest theory ever.

"Think about it. Who was this fellow who told you not to come over here? You said yourself that no one like that lives in Warrensburg. He's certainly not someone on the crew. And now, this new matter defies explanation. You were here and yet you weren't here.

William let that sink in, and then he said, slowly and dramatically, "I think some power is trying to destroy the movie. And it would appear to be a power that can take the form it chooses—including your form."

Nutty couldn't think of what to say. He didn't believe in ghosts. But he didn't have a better explanation.

By now Nutty's friends had spotted him, and they were coming over. Orlando Ortega yelled from some distance, "Hey, Nutty, I didn't know you could slug that hard. That guy was seeing stars."

And Charley "Bilbo" Blackhurst said, "You must have caught him when he wasn't expecting it."

"Naw, he probably paid the guy to take a fall," Orlando said. "He wants to change his wimpy image."

But Nutty was too worried to trade insults with Orlando this morning.

Mindy Marshall was right behind the boys. She said, "Oh, Orlando, don't be so stupid. Nutty may be slender, but he's strong."

Nutty had had about enough of Mindy. She had hated him all her life until she thought he was a movie star, and now she was hanging around him every minute she could.

Right now, however, he had bigger concerns. Someone was running around hitting people— someone who looked exactly like him.

But it was Richie Fetzer who said the worst thing possible. "Hey, I'm not surprised you hit that guy. You looked weird this morning—your eyes were all blurry or something, like you were really mad. I saw you come out of the makeup trailer, and I thought, wow, he looked like a ghost."

William nodded and mumbled, "He saw it too."

Nutty threw up his hands. "Come on, everybody," he said. "Don't talk like that."

But William suddenly grabbed Nutty's arm and pulled him aside. He whispered excitedly, "My whole life I've wondered whether ghosts really exist. I'd give almost anything to get some clear-cut proof, one way or the other. This could be my chance."

Nutty couldn't believe it. He had enough trouble with this . . . person—whatever it was. He didn't need William chasing the thing around— and thinking it was lots of fun.

But William was smiling. "This could turn out to be a real adventure," he said.

Nutty walked away.

He sat down on the lawn and cupped his forehead with his hand. He needed to think.

But the only thing that would come into his head was that he wished he hadn't gotten out of bed that morning.

Chapter 2

"All right. All right. Let's get on with it," Mr. Deveraux was shouting. *Damian* Deveraux, the director.

Nutty had learned from one of the crew members that the guy's real name was Frank Crandall. Somehow, that sounded more like it.

But now the great Deveraux was calling for another scene. He had given up on the fight scene because the big actor who had been hurt wasn't coming around very quickly.

Nutty had pulled on the overalls that his part called for, and he had gotten himself all dabbed up with heavy makeup. He really hated the stuff.

"All right now," Mr. Deveraux told Nutty and Sarah, "I want you to immerse yourselves in the mood of this scene. It's crucial, absolutely crucial. The entire film hinges on this moment when you two kiss each other for the very first time."

That's all Nutty needed this morning. He had known for a long time that he wouldn't mind, someday maybe, trying a kiss with Sarah. She was an awfully cute girl, and he had "liked" her for a long time. But in front of all these people? And after all he had been through already this morning?

Little Mr. Deveraux looked at Nutty intensely, his eyes like drops of tar. "Forget that you're Parker House," he told Nutty. "You are the boy who defended his family against the Hell's Cherubs gang. You're not even Hank Barley. You're the 'Tae Kwon Do Guy.' You *know* you can fight a whole army of tough guys."

Nutty had no trouble forgetting he was Parker House—or Hank Barley. But picturing himself as the Tae Kwon Do Guy, the title character of the movie, that was tough.

"All your life you've been nothing," Deveraux told him. "Worse than nothing. A clodhopper. A stupid farm boy with a straw in your mouth and a milk cow for a best friend."

Nutty knew kids who lived on farms, and they weren't at all like that. But it didn't do any good to tell Mr. Deveraux. Nutty had already learned his lesson on that one.

"But now. *Now.* You've taken Tae Kwon Do training, and you've become a spiritual man, a defender. What you have found in yourself is greatness. Deep, inner greatness. And this woman—

15

this innocent farm girl—senses who you are. She longs for your touch. She quivers with anticipation as she contemplates the velvety vibration of your lips on hers."

Nutty heard Orlando snicker, and he felt his own face get hot. Sarah ducked her head and turned bright red. This was the worst thing that had happened yet, and everything about this movie had been bad.

Up until now, the worst scenes had been the ones with Conway Pim, the wandering spiritual man and former baker, who had taught Hank Barley to lead a pure life—and to knock people around. The whole idea was that Hank had to knead bread dough sixteen hours a day. This strengthened his arms and hands and, at the same time, helped him know the meaning of life. "Bread is life, and dough is the means to make it," Mr. Deveraux had told Nutty.

Nutty had only found that it stuck to his fingers. He wasn't sure what that meant.

What bothered Nutty most was that people were actually going to enter theaters and see this dumb movie and watch Parker or Hank—or whoever he was—work up a sweat over a lump of dough.

"And so, Parker, this is the moment when you shed your skin. Do you understand? You sluff off your old self, and you become the you that you can be. This kiss is the symbol of the new you—tender . . . tough . . . powerful . . . meek. Everything in contrast, all that is *rough and wild*, and all that is *sooofffft* and *sweeeet*. Do you feel what I mean?"

Nutty didn't, but he said he did.

"Okay. Think yourself into the part, Parker. Let it fill you up. I want you to take five minutes. I want you to spend it staring into Mary Elizabeth's eyes. Forget where you are and who you are. Become the Tae Kwon Do Guy. Can you do that for me, Park? Can you give it your best shot—my man?"

"Sure."

"Oh, Park, I love you. I know I've been tough. But it's only because I want the best from you. Do you understand that?"

"Yeah." Nutty looked down at the ground. He could stand the guy angry—anytime—better than this.

"Okay. Wonderful. Now look into her eyes, and I'll take a break. When I come back, I want you to be a new person."

Off he went, on a trot. His hair—really a toupee—had a strange way of bouncing, like wings.

Nutty glanced over at his friends. They all had small parts in the movie. They played his buddies at school. They were dressed up in overalls today, but lately they had been showing up at the set in their new "Hollywood" styles. To Nutty's taste, that was a little much.

But right now all of them were grinning. They knew how much Nutty wanted to stare into Sarah's eyes while everyone watched. "Get ready for a big smacker," Orlando whispered.

"Shut up," Nutty said, and he looked back at Sarah, but not directly into her eyes.

"Nutty, you better do what he said," William said. "Who knows? It might help." William also had a part in the movie. One scene. Mostly, though, he stayed around the set to "represent" Nutty as his agent.

So Nutty looked into Sarah's eyes. She looked good too. She had a pretty smile, dimples and all, and she had nice eyes, very blue. Nutty usually didn't mind looking at her—but mainly when she didn't know it. Now she was staring right back at him.

Nutty lasted about ten seconds, and then he started to laugh. And when he did, so did Sarah. After that, every time their eyes met, they broke up.

And the guys watching only made it worse. Orlando whispered, "Nutty, don't put your *lips* on it!"

Sarah cocked her head to the side and said, "Don't you wish you could, Orlando?" But then, she instantly turned red.

18

All the guys laughed—including Nutty—and Richie said, "That's all Orlando dreams of. He wants a big slobbery one."

"Shut up!" Orlando growled, and he punched Richie in the shoulder.

Things kept going that way the whole time. Only one thing finally stopped them—and then not quite entirely—and that was the return of their brilliant director.

"All right. How did it go? Let me see your face, Park. Let me see the change."

Nutty looked at the man and tried to seem . . . something, maybe solemn.

"What's this?" Deveraux screamed. "That's some sort of smirk. You look like you stole a watermelon. You're supposed to be a man of love and war." He slammed his clipboard against his forehead, and then he stared into the sky. His lips moved, but nothing came out.

Nutty had no idea how to be a man of love and war. He could give either one a shot. But both—at the same time?

"All right," Mr. Deveraux finally said. "Let's try again. I swear I don't know why the world considers me a genius. I've failed to reach you, teach you, mold you. I've failed to get my vision into your eyes—your soul. But I'll not give up. Never!"

He tossed his clipboard away. It clattered

across a nearby sidewalk. He grabbed Nutty by both shoulders and drew him up close, so that their noses were not far from touching. "Parker, listen to me. Feel this. You are a fighter—a killer. But you don't kill, because deep down—deeper than the killer—is a lover. You care. Above all, you care about this woman."

But when Mr. Deveraux said "woman," Nutty made a very big mistake. He let the tiniest hint of a smile creep into the corners of his mouth. And when he did, Orlando laughed—just a little. But it was enough to make Nutty laugh.

And when he did that, Deveraux lost it. He leaped in the air and came down swearing—or maybe speaking in some other language. He babbled for at least a minute, and then, finally, he spun around and one clear word came out. "Meditate!" he shouted, and ran for his trailer.

That was Deveraux's answer for everything. Once he hit the boiling point, he did five minutes of his yoga—or whatever it was—and he usually came back sweet as pie. For a while.

All that was really nothing new. The only thing that was different was that Nutty and Sarah—and even the crew—were cracking up. And they had never had the nerve to do that before.

Nutty was actually feeling better.

And then he saw the big actor come out of his

trailer—the guy Nutty was supposed to have hit. He was the size of a rhino. And yet, he still seemed weak in the knees. Suddenly a sick feeling returned to Nutty's stomach. Who had actually hit the guy? He took a look around the set. Was there really a ghost out there somewhere?

He felt a shudder pass through him. This was not a great time to be trying to think about love and war—and kissing.

Mr. Deveraux soon got himself under control and came back. He said he couldn't let himself get that mad again—he was sorry. And he started all over.

He never got quite the look he wanted from Nutty, but he decided to give the scene a try. "Parker, Sarah," he said, "I'm going to roll the cameras. I have a feeling an innocent first kiss might work best when it is, indeed, a first kiss for the two of you." He stopped suddenly and focused in on them suspiciously. "You haven't already kissed each other, I hope?"

Nutty said, "I haven't kissed *anyone*." Nutty shot a quick glance at Orlando, who was still trying not to laugh.

"Wonderful. *Wonderful.* We're going to catch the miracle of your very first kiss, and we're going to get it on the first take. I feel this. Do you know your lines?"

"Uh, yeah, I think so."

"No, Parker, no. Don't take on that Hank Barley manner. You sound like the old Hank when you talk that way."

Nutty thought he was just being Nutty.

"All right. Let's run through the lines, but don't kiss her. We'll save that for the take."

That was good. But the lines were stupid. Not just stupid. They were in some new league of stupidity. Nutty had been dreading this scene ever since he had first read it.

Poor Hank had to say, "Mary Elizabeth, you are part of me—no, you are me, and I am you. We're one soul. We are the air, the sea, the wind in the trees, the color of ripe wheat, and the smell of earth—rich soil and strong manure."

And then he was supposed to pull her slowly to him, gaze into her eyes, and plant one on her.

Oh, man! How could he do this?

But he tried. He looked at Sarah and tried to be manly and tough, and sick with the flu at the same time. That was about as close as he could imagine to what Deveraux kept talking about.

But he no sooner got the "look" on his face than Deveraux demanded to know, "What's that? You look like you just sniffed a smelly sweat sock. This is the woman you love."

22

So Nutty tried to look a little more "in love."

"Better, better. Give me more. Commit yourself to it, Park. Go with that. Let it flow through you."

And so Nutty exaggerated the flu and left out the fighter stuff entirely.

"Yes. Yes. Yes. That's it. Oh, Parker, you're going to rise to greatness yet. All right. Let's have the lines."

"Mary Elizabeth," Nutty began, "you are part of me—no, you are me, and I am you. We're—"

"No, no, no. No!" And Damian Deveraux broke down. His voice cracked and tears spilled onto his cheeks. "Parker, please. Try. Don't say the lines. Emote them. Let them fall from your lips like honey from a dripper. Care, Parker. Care."

Nutty thought maybe he could go with the flu a little more. He tried to sound sick. Deveraux liked that better.

So Nutty went after the whole speech. He was plowing right along until he bogged down in the soil and manure.

He had never tried to stare into a girl's eyes while he gave a fluey speech about love. Still, he might have managed that. But talking to her about manure—well, that was too much for him.

The moment he started to laugh, so did Sarah. And so did all Nutty's buddies.

Deveraux threw a fit.

And, well . . . things only got worse from there.

But Nutty went back to the plow.

He kept trying the line—over and over and over—until he was so tired of it that he could say manure right into Sarah's face. And since the camera was looking at the back of her head, all Sarah had to do was hang in there with a blank look on her face.

Once Nutty got the lines sick enough, and could hold a straight face, Deveraux decided it was time to roll the camera again. Only about two hours had gone by since Nutty had first given the line a try.

"You'll do this right when you know that you're really going to kiss her," Deveraux said. "Let the anticipation spark you, and then let the kiss carry through you like electricity."

But the anticipation made Nutty nervous, not "electric." And after all the tries, and finally mucking his way through the manure, he forgot to wait and gaze. He just planted. He bonked his lips on top of Sarah's without thinking to turn his head one way or the other.

Noses smashed.

Orlando laughed.

Then Nutty did.

And then Sarah.

That's all Deveraux could take. "Cut! Cut!" he screamed. He threw himself flat on his face on the grass. He covered his head and lay there. Then, just as suddenly, he jumped up and called for a lunch break. "We'll get this right yet," he claimed. "Either that or I'll turn into a mass murderer."

And when he came back after lunch, he seemed more optimistic. But things didn't get better. Nutty got some kissing instructions, and that helped him arrange his nose, but he couldn't seem to resist puckering up and making a smack out of the kiss. And after two—maybe three—seconds, he would back off every time.

And that wouldn't do.

So Nutty spent the entire afternoon announcing his love in bad lines, and then landing bad kisses—the kind a boy gives his aunt. And Deveraux kept shouting, "Cut!" and then starting the scene all over.

Deveraux finally got him to unpucker, and then he pleaded, "Son, don't stretch your lips so tight. You make it look like a couple of billiard balls smacking into each other. Part your lips just a little and let them go soft and flabby."

Part his lips? Let them go flabby?

Gross!

Nutty glared at his friends and dared them to

laugh. They were all tired by now, however, and William said, "Just do it, Nutty. For crying out loud, haven't you watched how they kiss in the movies?"

But Nutty didn't do a whole lot better, and Sarah was beginning to look green. Stupid lines, bad kisses, and summer heat—it was not a good combination. At one point Sarah whispered to Nutty, "If we ever get through this, I'll never kiss anybody, ever again."

"Same here," Nutty said. "I feel like puking."

"Oh, yuck. Thanks a lot. That's just what I needed. It's bad enough to kiss you without you saying that."

"Hey, if you're such a great kisser, show me how."

"No thanks. I'll just go home and eat liver for supper. It has the same effect on me."

Nutty remembered when he used to like the girl—a few hours ago—but it seemed like ancient history now.

After twenty-two takes, and Nutty's voice going hoarse from all the manure talk, and his lips getting chappy from all the friction, Deveraux finally announced a "print."

Nutty couldn't believe it. He hadn't done any better than he had all day. But Deveraux hugged him and told him that he had "grown immensely," that he was now an actor.

Nutty didn't think so.

As Deveraux marched off into the sunset, Nutty was left standing in front of Sarah, who was exhausted.

"At least it's over," Nutty said.

Sarah let out a long sigh. "My lips feel like hamburger."

Nice image.

"Hey, you weren't stuck saying all those stupid lines."

But Sarah was not in a good mood. "Yeah, well, they were stupid before you got hold of them. And you made them stupider."

Nutty couldn't think of one thing to say—mainly because he knew she was right. But it still made him mad. Finally he growled, "Oh, yeah?"

And even Sarah couldn't think of a good response to that intelligent line. The two of them turned on their heels and walked away from each other.

It had been a very long day.

Nutty just wanted to . . .

And then, suddenly, he was on his face.

He hadn't tripped. He hadn't fallen. Something had knocked him down.

But he rolled over quickly and looked up.

Nothing was there.

Chapter 3

Nutty had made up his mind. He was not going to believe the possibility of a ghost. It wasn't possible, so he wasn't going to think about it. He made a conscious decision to think about his other little problem: that his life was ruined.

"William," he asked, "do you think *The Tae Kwon Do Guy* will be the worst movie in the history of the world?"

"Well, let me think," William answered, and he considered for a time. "I can't think of a worse one. But then, I don't go to all that many movies."

"I'll bet it will be at least in the bottom ten."

"I would say so. And who knows, with a few more scenes like the one you did today, you might be able to do it."

"Do what?"

"Hit the bottom—of the bottom."

"Thanks, William."

"Don't mention it."

The boys were walking home from the day's shooting, and they were shot. What an experience! The day of Nutty's first kiss—in fact the day of his first twenty-two kisses. And now he hoped never to kiss again. At least not Sarah.

"Look at it this way, Nutty. You're going to make enough money to put you through college, with enough left over to get a pretty good start in life."

"Yeah, and I also don't have to worry about making another movie. By the time people see this one, and laugh themselves sick, no one will ever want me to act again."

"I don't know about that, Nutty. A lot of famous actors got their starts in bad films. And poor acting ability usually doesn't stop people. At least not if they're cute, like you."

"Thanks, William. You've made me feel a whole lot better." But Nutty didn't really care what William said. All he wanted right now was to go home and rest for a while.

William had other things on his mind. "Nutty, have you ever tried to hit anybody with all your force?"

"Once I got so mad at Orlando I punched him."

"As hard as you could?"

"I don't know. I guess so."

"Did he fall down?"

"No."

"So if you couldn't knock down Orlando, the chances seem very slim that you could flatten a great big man."

"Especially if I was out at Pertle Springs at the time."

"Yes. But I'm wondering about some sort of dual existence, some transmigration of essences, or an illusion caused by—"

"Lay off, William. I don't even care. Whatever you guys saw this morning, all I know is that it wasn't me. And my dad can tell you where I was at the time."

"Yet, dozens of people saw someone. We all thought that it was you. And at the same time, some of us noticed a strange alteration in your eyes. I don't want to jump to any rash conclusions, but how do we explain such extraordinary events?"

"We don't, William. We hope the whole movie is a bad dream and will be gone in the morning."

"I suppose even that is possible. After all we've witnessed in the last few days, why couldn't the whole experience be a nightmare that isn't even happening? It's a fascinating possibility."

Nutty didn't think so. It was all so weird he

couldn't think what to make of it, and he was too tired to make sense anyway.

But William was still going strong. "Set off against that possibility, my ghost theory doesn't sound so farfetched, does it?"

"Not if you say so, William."

Nutty was happy when he got home. Once away from William, he promised himself to forget the whole thing. The problem was, it wasn't that easy. William's questions lingered in his mind.

At dinner, when his dad asked him what in the world had happened that morning, Nutty said, "It was some kind of mix up. We shot the scene in front of the school, the way Mr. Deveraux had planned all along."

He really didn't want to say more than that to his family. They would want him to explain everything, and he couldn't do that.

"So who was this fellow who told you to go to Pertle?"

"I don't know. But he got it all wrong."

"Was he on the crew, or—"

"Dad, I just don't know."

"Well, don't be so cranky. You're not such a big star that you can start that stuff with us."

Susie, Nutty's little sister, was quick to jump on that one. "He's mad because he's not a star, Dad. He's the worst actor who ever acted in the history of all acting. All the kids in the movie say so."

Nutty didn't fight back. Every word was true—even if it did come from his "cutey-pie," curly-haired nine-year-old sister. He didn't like knowing that kids were talking about it, but it didn't matter. Once the movie came out, his life was ruined anyway.

"Susie, don't be so cruel," Mrs. Nutsell said. "How do you think that makes Nutty feel?"

Susie shot a quick glance at Nutty, and then back at her mom. "Feel? Does Nutty have *feelings*?"

"That's not funny," Dad said. "Of course he does. And don't call him 'Nutty.' I hate that."

Nutty had no fight left in him. He didn't even threaten to kill his lovely sister. He only mumbled, "She's right, Dad."

"What?"

"She's right. I'm the worst actor of all time."

Mr. Nutsell pointed at Susie. "See. See what you've done. You've hurt him. Someday your brother is going to be so rich you'll want to be his friend. Then you'll be sorry you've been so unkind."

"Yeah, right," Susie said, and she giggled.

Mom said, "What's wrong, Freddie, did you have a bad day?"

But Nutty didn't want to talk about that either. If he told them he'd spent the whole day kissing Sarah, Susie would only make things worse. And so he only said, "Yeah, I guess," and then he added, "I'm going to bed early, okay?"

"But aren't you going to Susie's piano recital?"

"Let's see," Nutty answered, "let me think that one over. That's a really tough one." He put his hand to his chin and pretended to think for a moment. And then he said, "Uh . . . no! I think I'll pass on that one. After bad acting all day, I don't need bad piano."

He paid no attention when Susie told him to drop off the planet. He got up from the table.

What did cross his mind was that he hated to go anywhere in public anymore. Maybe a lot of people were talking about his lousy acting, but a lot more seemed to think he was the local celebrity, and they all had to have his autograph. Every kid in town knew that Nutty was also Parker House, the movie star. Some of them would actually follow him around. A girl named Rene had started writing love letters to him.

Nutty didn't need that. He knew he was going to go from big star to big flop as soon as the movie appeared. Otherwise, maybe it wouldn't have been so bad.

So Nutty went to his room and lay down on

his bed. The one luxury his dad had let him buy with the money from the movie was a TV for his room. He punched the remote to turn it on, and then he settled back for anything that was on. He made up his mind not to work on his lines. Practice didn't help him anyway.

He lasted about five minutes watching TV before he was sound asleep.

He slept soundly for quite some time.

And then something very strange began to happen.

Nutty felt some uneasiness that began to lift him from the depths of sleep. He moved his arm across his eyes, aware of light. He had gone to sleep without the lights on, but now something was there—some sound, some light. Yet, the clock in his head told him that it was not morning, that he hadn't been asleep all night.

For a couple of minutes Nutty was only half-awake, and he wished the light away. He heard words—whispered words—but he willed them out of his head. They were low vibrations, the shape of words, but the meaning wouldn't sink in. Still, he felt himself stirring, rising to consciousness, and he felt fear spreading over him like a cold draft.

Some defense within him said, "You're just dreaming this. Don't pay any attention." He felt the words now, knew what they meant, but he kept pushing them away.

"I warn you. I warn you," the voice kept saying, low and hard. "I warn you."

And finally Nutty couldn't keep them out.

"I warn you."

Suddenly he sat straight up. "What?" he said. "Who said that?"

He stared into the dark. He saw a strange, vague light. It was a green sort of glow, unmoving, near the door to his room.

"I warn you," came the whisper, almost like the sound of wind against the house.

Nutty blinked and tried to see, but his eyes were adjusting. And then everything was dark again.

Nutty was still sitting, still trying to think what was going on. He remembered the words, and he repeated them in his mind, but at the same time, he was trying to remember the shape. He had seen a person, maybe a man, tall and bony, with elbows sticking out. Or something of that sort. Green and glowing.

No!

He told himself he had seen nothing, heard nothing. Sometimes, at night, the house made strange sounds—or the wind. But he heard no wind now. Sometimes light could reflect, and sleepy eyes could turn them into shapes.

It was nothing.

He remembered the man on the street from that morning. The man with the strange clothes. This thing he had seen—hadn't its hips been rounded? Hadn't it worn those same strange pants?

No!

He had been dreaming. That was it. Stuff like that didn't happen. Voices in the night. Strange figures in the dark. He had been dreaming, for sure. But hadn't he looked right at the light? Hadn't he sat up and opened his eyes and looked? And hadn't he seen something? What kind of dream was that?

Still, it had to be a dream. That was the only explanation.

And so he flopped back on his bed. He realized by then that he still had his clothes on. He had never undressed or gotten under the covers. He didn't care. It was a warm night, even with the air conditioner running. And he didn't want to bother to get up.

And so he drifted back to sleep, or something close to it. But the voice was soon back, this time louder, this time vibrating in its depth through the room, like the bass tones in his stereo speakers— and yet harsher, more intense.

"Parker. Parker. I warn you."

Nutty sat up again. He blinked, hard. He tried to see what there was to see.

And this time he was sure of it. The man. The thin body, and the short, rounded pants. He could even see the long hair.

"I warn you," the voice said, suddenly clear, not whispered. "Do not return to the set in the morning. I warn you."

The shape was coming more clear all the time. It was the man. It was definitely him. The man he had seen on the street that morning. The man who had sent him to Pertle. Nutty was frozen.

"Do you understand?"

But Nutty wasn't talking to this guy. Something told him that it wasn't wise to admit the thing was real. The dream theory was still easier to live with. Yes, he was dreaming. He would wake up. Soon.

"Do you understand?" the voice demanded again, and then the skinny form took a step toward him.

"Yeah. Yeah. I understand."

Blink.

And the thing was gone.

The room was dark again. Except not quite dark, and Nutty knew that either morning was coming or it was still twilight. Something told him that the evening light was still fading. It must be only ten o'clock or so. He had a very long wait until morning. And now he wasn't sleepy. He didn't want to shut his eyes again and maybe call back the . . . figure.

The ghost?

He got up and hurried to the light switch by the door. He turned the light on, and then he looked around the room. But he was shaking all over, and he hurried back to his bed, where he could sit with a wall against his back and face the whole room in the light.

He tried to think. This time he had been awake. He just couldn't deny that. And he had definitely seen something. He had heard the voice. He had been warned. And the voice had asked him whether he had understood.

It wasn't a dream. So now what?

And then something else hit him. He had gone to sleep with the TV on. He was sure of it. And now it was off. Had one of his parents come in and turned it off? Possibly. But he hadn't heard anyone.

He looked at his watch. It was only 9:40. His parents were still up. He had to know.

So Nutty wandered down the hallway and found his dad and mom in the living room, both of them reading. "Dad, did you come in and turn my TV off?"

"No."

"What about you, Mom?"

"No. I was going to come down and check on you, but—"

"Are you sure? Are both of you absolutely sure you didn't turn my TV off?"

"Freddie, what are you talking about?" Mom asked. "Of course we're sure. We just got home a little while ago, and we didn't—"

"Where's Susie?"

"She's in the family room watching TV. But Freddie, she didn't go anywhere near your room. What's the matter with you, anyway? Why would anyone want to turn your TV off?"

"I was asleep."

"Well, then," Dad said, "I would think you would appreciate it, and not go around accusing everyone."

Nutty realized how he must sound—angry, or grouchy, or something. His parents didn't know how scared he was.

"No, it's not that. I just need to know for sure. You didn't—and Susie didn't—come into my room at all?"

"No, Freddie," Dad said. "We told you that."

And Mom added, "We've both been sitting right here. If Susie had gone down your hallway, we would have noticed."

Nutty stood there for a moment, still feeling as though he had just jumped out of a bad dream and hadn't landed quite square. And then he did the only thing he could think to do. He walked into the kitchen, picked up the phone, and dialed.

"Hello, is William there?" he said. And in a few seconds William was on the phone. "William, can you come over here *right now?*"

"Well it's getting a little late. I doubt my parents would let me do that."

"You can sleep over."

"Sleep over? Nutty I really don't think so. I—"

"William, the ghost was here."

"What?"

"A ghost was in my room. I saw him. He talked to me."

"I'll be right there."

Click.

Chapter 4

"Oh, my," William kept saying as he heard the story. When he heard about the ghostly light and the whispered words, he leaned back in his chair and said, "This is fantastic!"

The clincher came when Nutty told William about the TV and checking with his parents to see whether they had turned it off. "Physical evidence," William said. "Better yet. Wonderful!" He pulled out a little notepad from his pants pocket and a pen from his shirt pocket, and he began to write something down.

"No, William," Nutty said. "Not wonderful. We're talking about a ghost—or something like that. And he's warning me. That's not wonderful."

"Oh, I know, Nutty. Pardon me for seeming insensitive to your obvious concerns. But just think of it. If we could photograph it, or get it on audiotape, just think of the scientific implications!"

"Yeah, well, those are big words, but what if the thing knocks me off or something? Just think about that too!"

"Yes, well, that is one of the matters we must consider. But I really doubt that he intends any direct bodily damage to you. It sounds mostly as though he would rather use scare tactics—all this theatrical whispering and glowing, and that sort of thing."

"I don't care, William. I'm not going to the movie set in the morning. I'm quitting the movie. I'm sick of acting anyway."

"Now, Nutty, don't make your mind up quite yet. Let's think this through. I admit that you're not much of an actor, but—"

"William, I'm a horrible actor."

"Well, okay. You are quite horrible."

"Thanks." Nutty crashed onto his bed. Right now he was a lot more concerned with the ghost than he was with his "acting career," but it wasn't much fun to remember that disaster either.

"Now, now. Don't get your feelings hurt. Just count your money and forget the Academy Awards."

"Very funny."

"Nutty, look at all this from another point of

42

view. This is a moment in history. Wouldn't you like to be part of the team that revealed to the world, once and for all, that ghosts actually exist?"

Nutty sat up. "William, if some guy had a gun pointed at you, would you want to be the first guy to prove that you could bounce bullets off your head?"

"Well, now, it's nothing like that. We can prove how hard your head is later." He chuckled, but Nutty didn't. "Right now we need to lie in wait for this ghost."

William was moving into deep concentration. Nutty knew that look very well. It usually came just before William got one of his "big" ideas. It also usually came just before Nutty found himself in big trouble.

William was sitting on Nutty's desk chair, which he had turned around, and he was leaning back, gazing off into outer space—or maybe at the ceiling.

A couple of minutes went by, and Nutty tried to use the time to think. Maybe he could sneak away in the night and spend some time at his grandparents' house. They might cover for him, so Deveraux wouldn't find him. And the ghost might not bother with him so long as he didn't go near the set.

"Nutty, here's what I'm thinking," William suddenly announced. "You have nothing to fear."

"Right. That's what you always tell me."

"When have I ever told you that before?"

"Well, there was the time you stuck my head in that black box and got those photon things after me. You kept saying—"

"Well, sure. But that was an entirely different sort of thing. Think it through logically. If the ghost wanted to get to you, he could have done that anytime he wanted to. He obviously has some other purpose. Today, he apparently had you sent in the wrong direction—and then he appeared, disguised as you, and did something to delay filming for the day."

"Yeah, and he knocked me down. And he slugged a big guy hard enough to knock his socks off."

"Sure. But he didn't really do any permanent damage. It was a mere delaying tactic. All of his tricks have been the same sort of thing. People fall down, cameras malfunction, the microphones don't pick up—that sort of stuff. And now this very showy appearance of his, after all is said and done, was only a warning to stay away for the day and delay production again."

"That's right. And it worked. I'm not going."

"And play right into his hands?"

"Yup. He can have what he wants from me. The dude is scary."

"Really? Did you see his facial features, or get some sense of what sort of man he was?"

"Not really. But when I saw him on the street, he looked like—"

"What?"

"You know—when I saw him this morning, and he told me to go to Pertle Springs."

"Nutty! You didn't tell me that before. You think he's the same man who misguided you?"

"Maybe. He was skinny, and he had long hair, and I think he had the same kind of weird pants on."

"That is interesting. Very interesting. And it reminds me of the other possibility—the one I hate to admit."

"What, William? Just tell me. Don't talk in riddles."

"You seem awfully irritable, Nutty."

"William, a ghost was in my room tonight. Don't tell me I'm irritable. What would you be?"

"Well, that's just the point I was about to make. I've let myself become quite unscientific. I sort of like the idea of discovering a ghost. But the truth is, all the things that happened on the set could be a mere break of bad luck. And this thing that happened to you tonight is starting to sound more and more like a dream."

"No way, William. I was wide-awake. At least the second time I was."

"I know it seemed so. But you saw this strange fellow this morning, and then I plant the suggestion in your mind that a ghost is running around. So you go to bed, and perhaps quite naturally, you have a dream about the man you saw, and in the dream he turns into a ghost."

"Yeah, and what about the TV?"

"I was just thinking about that. In the first place, you might have been falling asleep and decided to push the OFF button on the remote—and you just don't remember it because you were so sleepy. Or you could even have rolled over on it."

"Uh-uh. I don't buy that. I saw the guy."

"Okay, good. I hope so. But let's just hang on and not pass judgment until we have better evidence. I'll stay with you tonight, and see whether I see anything. And in the morning let's go to the set and see whether anything happens."

"William, I don't get you. This morning you were sure there was a ghost, and now you're telling me I had a dream."

"I know. But if we're going to prove the existence of the ghost, we have to have clear-cut evidence."

Nutty thought about it. Finally he said, "Well, let's try to get through the night first, and worry about the rest in the morning."

"Fine. Fair enough. Do you have a sleeping bag

or some blankets I can use? I'll sleep right here on the floor, close to you."

What comfort. William would probably make friends with the guy if he showed up again.

But Nutty got out some bedding for William, and then the two tried to get to sleep. The problem was, Nutty wasn't sleepy now. He lay awake for a long time.

William was soon taking long, deep breaths that began to sound dangerously close to a snore.

A lot of help he was going to be!

Time passed very slowly, and Nutty was beginning to think he never would go to sleep. And then he realized that he had dozed off for a time, and something was happening. The whisper was in his head again, the words.

"I warn you."

"No," Nutty muttered, and then he came fully awake. He sat up, and he saw the green glow again.

"William. William!" he whispered, but William's steady breathing didn't even pause.

"I warn you," the voice said. "Don't go to the set today."

This time the form had taken clear shape. It was the man. The same man. Nutty was sure of it. And he *wasn't* dreaming.

"William!"

Nothing.

"Do you understand?" the man asked.

But Nutty wanted William to see this. He didn't want to face the thing alone.

"William!"

And finally Nutty heard some stirring on the floor.

"Do you understand?"

And again the man, green but clear, stepped toward the bed. At the same moment, Nutty dove. He landed right on top of William, who grunted and then, in his confusion, yelled, "Get off me! Get off me!"

"Look! Look! He's here!" Nutty was screaming, but William had managed to get his arm around Nutty's neck and he began to squeeze.

"Leave me alone!" William was screaming, and yet he had locked onto Nutty like a vise.

"Wake up. It's me!" Nutty was yelling at the same time. "The ghost is here. Look at him."

By now William seemed to be making some sense of the situation. "Nutty," he gasped, as though he had finally realized what it was he had locked in his arm. But he didn't let his grip loosen.

"Let go of me, William," Nutty grunted. "You're breaking my neck."

"Why'd you do that?" William said, and yet he sounded relieved. He let go of Nutty and fell back on the floor.

"Look at me—" But Nutty looked around and saw that nothing was there. The light was gone.

"What in the world were you trying—"

"William, you missed it. The ghost was here."

William sat straight up. "What? Where?"

"It was by the door. It said the same stuff again. You slept right through it."

"Are you sure?"

"Yeah, I'm sure, and it was not a dream. I saw the thing standing right by—"

But just then the door flew open. For a moment, Nutty thought the ghost was making a return, and he cringed, but the light came on, and his mother was standing in the doorway in her nightgown, staring at William and Nutty. They were both still sprawled on the floor.

"What in the world is going on?" she said.

"Mom, it was a ghost. A real ghost," Nutty said.

"What?"

Nutty sat up. "A ghost was in this room. He warned me. He said—"

"What?"

"I told you—"

But just then Mr. Nutsell appeared in nothing but a pair of blue-striped boxer shorts. He looked confused, with his hair hanging in his eyes and his skinny, white, hairy legs sticking out from his underwear. "What in the world?" he said, but he couldn't seem to find the words to complete his question.

Suddenly William bounced to his feet. He stood there in his green jammies with the little frog embroidered on the front, and he told the biggest lie Nutty had ever heard. "Excuse us, Mr. and Mrs. Nutsell, let me explain what I think just happened. Nutty apparently had a nightmare and sort of went hysterical. He must have jumped out of bed and tripped over me. I was sleeping here on the floor."

"Oh, for heaven's sake, Freddie," Mom said. "You scared me half to death."

"But he's not telling the truth, Mom. It was a ghost. I mean a real, one hundred percent, honest-to-goodness ghost. I'm not making it up. He was all green and glowy, and he sort of whispered when he talked, and he said, '*I warn you.*'" Nutty made the whispering sound he remembered.

William shrugged and smiled, and then said, "You know how real a dream can seem sometimes."

Mr. Nutsell nodded and wandered away. He didn't seem entirely awake. Mrs. Nutsell said, "Freddie, get back to bed. I think you're letting this movie upset you, and it's causing you nightmares. I'll leave the door open and the hall light on." And she left too.

She believed William instead of her own beloved son. It was crazy. Nutty jumped up and stood nose-to-nose with William. "What are you talking about? I *saw* it again. I *know* I wasn't dreaming."

"Yes, sure. Maybe. But I knew your parents weren't likely to believe it. Or if they did, they wouldn't want you to go to the set in the morning."

Nutty's face turned into a goldfish imitation. His eyes bulged. His mouth hung open. "William, I'm finished with all this. I've seen that guy three times, and I don't want to see him again."

"Yes, I can imagine. But if it wasn't a dream, somehow we have to find a way to prove it."

Nutty slumped to the floor and dropped his head into his hands. He didn't know there were messes this big—let alone that he could be the one in the middle.

Chapter 5

The next day Nutty found himself walking with William to the set in front of the school. What Nutty didn't know was *why* he was walking with William to the set in front of the school.

William had talked and talked, and Nutty had finally given in, but William's talk hadn't really convinced him. Nutty's biggest problem was that he didn't dare tell his dad that he wanted to drop out of the movie.

And maybe the other trouble was, Nutty was wondering himself, now that it was daylight. Maybe it really had been a dream. Or three dreams.

But that didn't mean he wasn't scared. What did "I warn you" mean? More scares would be bad enough. But this ghost could also *punch*, according to all the witnesses. And no one said that little episode was a dream.

When Nutty arrived at the school, it wasn't a ghost that he saw. It was Orlando in a pair of shades, and his hair all slicked back. "Orlando," Nutty said, "what happened to you?"

"Hey, do you like it?" he answered, and he ran the palm of his hand over his hair. "I'm going to a new hair stylist."

"Stylist? You gotta be kidding."

"Hey, no way. My barber didn't know one thing about style. This new guy made me look like this." Orlando struck a pose—his head cocked back, and one hand tucked into his pants pocket.

"Well, I suppose you could sue him," William said.

"Hey, what are you talking about? I'm looking *good*, man. I'm getting an agent too. A real one. My dad says I can be a bigger star than Nutty—because I'm better looking."

"Yeah, you are better looking than some movie stars," Nutty said. "Like maybe . . . the Ninja Turtles."

"Very funny, Nutty. You just wait and see what I do."

Orlando had been jealous from the beginning. He played Nutty's best friend, which gave him a couple more lines than Bilbo or Richie—or in other words, a total of three.

"Orlando, you can't act any better than I can,"

Nutty said. "Neither one of us should ever be in a movie again."

Nutty tried to walk away. He was a lot more concerned about what might happen today than he was about Orlando's jealousy.

"Nutty, you're nuts. Every girl in town wants to go with you. Pretty soon it'll be all the girls in the country."

"Since when do you care about girls?"

"Since I grew up, man."

Brother! Just when Nutty was losing interest in girls Orlando was catching on to the idea.

Nutty noticed Richie and Bilbo getting out of a car. Both were wearing sunglasses and loose-looking shirts that were buttoned all the way to the neck.

Nutty had on an old pair of jeans, and he had grabbed his oldest T-shirt. He was never going to worry about *styles*. When would these guys give up the Hollywood bit?

Richie walked up and said, "Hey, dude, what's happening?"

"I don't know. It must be Halloween."

"By the way, Nutty," Orlando said, "you're the worst kisser I've ever seen. You gotta learn what to do with your nose, man."

"Yeah, like you know. How many girls have you kissed?"

"Plenty."

"Yeah? Name a few."

"Hey, I don't kiss and tell."

"You don't kiss and *anything*."

"Well, I know this much. You do it like this." Orlando pretended to take a girl in his arms and swing her back. Then he pressed his parted, sagging lips against an imaginary female and wagged his head slowly back and forth.

"That's sick, Orlando," Nutty said. "You get her spit in your mouth that way."

Nutty's buddies all cracked up about that. "A little spit won't hurt you," Richie said, and he nudged Bilbo. "Tell Sarah to suck on a Cert. It turns her spit into fruit juice."

"Oh, yuck!" Nutty said. "Lay off, will you, Richie?"

"Nutty, you don't know the first thing about girls *or* kissing," Orlando told him. "You better work on your techniques before all of us guys beat you out for the best parts."

"So is that what you guys think? You're all going to be movie stars—and all be hot with the girls?"

"I've always been hot," Orlando said. "I'm just getting ready to sizzle."

Nutty didn't get a chance to tell Orlando what he thought of his future in the movies. Mr. Deveraux pulled up in his limousine and immediately began screaming. "Why aren't you performers in costume? We need to make up for lost time today."

So the "performers" hurried off to the makeup trailer and got themselves ready. They were shooting a group scene this morning. Nutty—or that is, Hank—had to tell his good buddies how much they meant to him—in his "deepest soul."

Gag!

The scene was at a private meeting place, in front of a rock wall. The Hell's Cherubs were supposed to jump down on them. But the movie crew hadn't found a real rock wall, with a ledge, like the one the plot called for. So Deveraux had ordered one built.

The only trouble was, the wall had a mind of its own. It was constructed in two sections, but the connection wouldn't fit. And then, once the carpenters forced the thing together, it didn't want to stand up.

And that was only the beginning. One delay followed another. Electrical problems. Camera problems. You name it.

"Do you think it's the ghost?" Nutty whispered to William.

William had been trying to help Nutty work on his part, but now he looked up at the wall. "Possibly," he said. "But let's not assume anything."

"They stuck it together yesterday and it worked fine," Nutty said. "But I was watching just now, and it looked like someone had knocked some two-by-fours out of place."

"Well, as I say—maybe. But let's keep our scientific objectivity, and just wait to see what happens."

"Hey, William, don't tell me what to think. I'm the one who has to take the chances."

"All I'm saying is—"

"All you're saying is to watch and see if I get my head knocked off. Then we'll really have some good proof."

"Nutty, don't worry. I won't leave your side."

"Right. If we stick together, we can beat the Hell's Cherubs. You know it in your deepest soul. I'm not sure which one of these scripts is stupider."

"Nutty, what's with you this morning? I've never seen you so grouchy."

But Nutty didn't answer. He wasn't sure himself. He did know that a lot of other people—Deveraux, his dad, William—were making his decisions for him. And he was getting tired of it.

After half a morning of problems, Deveraux finally called the actors onto the set. "At last we're ready," he said. "But I see no reason for numerous takes. This is a simple, tender scene. Parker, just let the words flow from your heart."

"Mr. Deveraux."

It was Orlando. Deveraux looked at him with disgust, as though he had let out a huge belch. "What?" he said. He didn't like to have anyone say very much—except for himself, of course.

Orlando ran his hand over his slicked-back hair, as if he wanted Deveraux to notice, and then he said, "I've been reading these lines over, and I was thinking, when Nutty says . . ." Orlando found the place in the script and read, " 'Buddies, no matter what happens, no matter what dangers we face, I want you to know that you are the finest friends a young man ever had, the swellest pals in the world. And I love you, warmly and everlastingly. Know that, my good buddies. Know that forever.' "

"Yes, yes," Deveraux spouted, and he seemed annoyed. Orlando's reading didn't do the lines a lot of good.

"Well, I was thinking. Probably a guy wouldn't say all that stuff to his friends. At least, not quite that much, or that long. But see, you could cut it in half. Then his best friend could say half of the stuff back to him, and—"

"You just want a bigger piece of the action," Deveraux barked. "I wrote those lines with tears running down my cheeks. No one will take them away from my star."

"Yeah, well, it was just a thought," Orlando

said, and he slipped back behind Bilbo and Richie.

Nutty was tempted to laugh, but he didn't dare. He knew what Deveraux would think of that. He was also still sort of depressed from hearing Orlando read the lines.

But Deveraux was rebuilding the "spirit" now, pleading with Nutty to express his heart and soul. "Get inside the words, Parker," he begged, "and let the meanings—more than the syllables—flow off your tongue."

Nutty tried. He tried, with a straight face, to tell Bilbo and Orlando and Richie (whose script names were Roy, Buck, and Bud) how much he loved them. But the "heart and soul" seemed to stick in his throat.

Deveraux punted his clipboard like a football. "Why?" he screamed. "Why do I have to put up with this?"

Then he tried again. He pleaded with Parker, called him "son" and "sweetheart." "Please, please," he begged. "Reach inside yourself. Speak love. If you don't, I swear . . . I'll pull your tongue out by the roots."

Nutty knew he had to give it his best shot.

He overacted the lines so badly that crew members had to cover their mouths to keep from laughing. He was halfway through the destruction, however, when his own sense of personal worth must have jumped up and said, "Stop. Enough!"

Or maybe he just forgot his part.

Deveraux was patient. "That's all right," he said. "You were wonderful that time. Absolutely perfect. Just take a look at your lines again, get into them, and do the whole thing."

Nutty went after the lines again. He knew it was wrong—disgusting, embarrassing—but he went ahead, just to get it over with.

He looked into the eyes of his friends—who were trying hard not to laugh—and began the speech. "Buddies, no matter—"

But Richie had started to smile, and Nutty had to duck his head.

"Cut!" Deveraux yelled. "That's all right, Park. Tell me when you're ready. Get yourself together. I know you're feeling a lot of emotion right now."

At least he hadn't seen that Nutty had been about to laugh.

"Okay. I'm ready now," Nutty said, and he looked back at his friends—except that he actually picked a spot on Bilbo's shoulder to look at, so he wouldn't see their faces.

"Take three. And . . . roll."

"Buddies, no matter what happens, no matter what dangers we face, I want you to know that you are the finest friends a young man ever—"

Crack!

"Look out!"

Nutty's friends all scrambled backwards. Nutty wasn't sure what was happening, but he dove and rolled.

And right behind him, the set—the rock wall—crashed on the ground with a huge thud.

Nutty found himself facedown on the grass. He blew out the air that had caught in his chest.

William jumped down next to him. "Are you all right?"

"Yeah. I think so."

"I think our ghost has made his move."

Nutty had to wonder what might have happened to him had the wall caught him on the head. The ghost was getting down to serious business now.

"On the other hand," William added, "that wall was badly built. We still don't have any real proof."

"How about if he had killed me? Would that do it?"

"It would depend on how he did it," William said, and he chuckled. "But really, I doubt he would do anything like that."

Nutty rolled over on his back. "Good, William. Your doubt means a lot to me. You're the swellest pal in the whole world."

Orlando had come over now. "I thought *I* was," he said, and he grinned. "Hey, that was close. I wish those idiot carpenters could do something right."

Nutty sat up, and then he cupped his hands against the sides of his head. "I wish the thing had broken my legs. Then I could get out of this stupid movie."

"Hey, that's a good idea Nutty. Then a real actor could take over."

Nutty looked up to see Orlando smoothing back his hair again. Nutty was about to tell him what he thought when William said, "Nutty, come with me for a minute."

When Nutty stood up, he finally paid attention to all the fuss that was going on. Deveraux and his crew were trying to figure out what had gone wrong. Not one of them even asked Nutty whether he was all right.

William was pulling on Nutty's arm, so the two of them walked away from everyone. William's forehead was wrinkled, the way it always got when he was doing some hard thinking.

"Nutty," he said, "we must figure this ghost out—determine what it is he wants. Do you remember anything else about him?"

"Not really. I told you what he looked like."

Nutty didn't really have his mind on the question. He was thinking a lot more about what he should do. It was starting to sink in that not only he, but a lot of other people could have been hurt.

"Think, Nutty. Is there anything you've left out? Anything about his clothes? Anything he said?"

"No, William. I've told you everything. I don't see why you . . . oh—"

"What?"

"When I saw him on the street, he did tell me his name."

"His *name*? For crying out loud, Nutty. You should have told me. What was it?"

Nutty sat up. "It was . . . the same as . . ." Nutty tried to get back the connection that had registered in his mind. "It was something you eat. Something . . ."

"Like what? A meat? A salad? Dessert? What?"

"Be quiet for a minute. Let me think."

And then the connection came back. A cracker. "Oh, yeah. Graham. Matthew Graham. He said it like it was four words. 'Math—hew Gray—ham at your service,' he told me."

"Nutty, you should have told me that in the beginning."

"Why? Do you know him?"

"No, but I'll look into it. It could be very important."

"Maybe it's just a name he made up."

"Yes, maybe. But it still could be a clue."

Chapter 6

r. Deveraux soon realized that the wall could not be repaired quickly. He decided not to lose the whole day. He ordered the crew to set up in the school kitchen.

He would shoot a scene in which Conway Pim, the wandering Tae Kwon Do guru, would talk to Hank Barley about the meaning of bread dough and life. Both needed kneading and needing—according to the script—and both would rise if you left them alone. Or something like that. Nutty never really got the idea.

Still, he tried to be Hank, and he listened to Conway talk about instilling dough and the world with power, like yeast. But inside Hank was Nutty, kneading the heck out of a ball of dough, and needing like heck to get out of there. His hands and wrists ached, and his head hurt from the lights and the stupidity.

But on and on the shoot continued. Deveraux kept demanding more and more takes, so that Conway could "find the perfect balance between philosophy and bakery," the "kernel of the wheat and of the truth."

Poor Conway, an actor by the name of Brando Brittania (who's real name, he had once admitted to Nutty, was Mervin Thurman), had no more idea what Deveraux wanted than anyone else did. He finally gave up and played the part as though he were doing a death scene in a melodrama, and Deveraux got excited and said that was it—and only asked for seven more takes before he called the scene "perfect."

Nutty finally got to go home.

He usually walked home with William, but William had apparently gotten weary and left.

As Nutty walked home, he remembered, rather happily, that no one was at his house. His mom and dad had promised to take Susie into Kansas City to do some shopping. That meant he wouldn't have to discuss the movie—the disaster—with his dad that night.

But when Nutty got the key from the hiding place on the back porch and let himself into his house, he felt strange. The angle of the evening sun left the house dismal and eerie. He switched on the kitchen light and checked to see what he could eat.

His mom had left a note that his supper was in the microwave, and that he should reheat it. He gave the food a blast for a couple of minutes, and then he took the plate into the family room. He switched on the TV, and he sat down and ate.

After a few minutes, the silly sitcom that was showing could not take Nutty's mind off the strange feeling that had come over him. He really wished that his mom and dad were home after all.

And then he heard a noise.

He suddenly went rigid. He waited and listened.

Someone—or something—was in the house. He had heard something bump on a wall or on a floor. He couldn't tell exactly where it had come from, but he thought it might have been in the hallway, or in one of the bedrooms.

Nutty told himself that it might have been one of those noises that a house makes, or maybe the wind had blown a tree limb against the house. But he knew better. Something had moved inside the house. He had heard a little collision.

Of course, sometimes something in a closet shifted or fell, just pulled by gravity and vibrations in the house. It could be something like that. Most things could be explained once you checked them out—without jumping to a lot of crazy conclusions. That's what William always said.

But Nutty still couldn't move, couldn't eat—really, couldn't think very well.

And no matter what he tried to tell himself, something kept saying, "That ghost is in my house with me, and I'm here alone."

If only William had come home with him. What was with the guy anyway? This morning he was all hot to catch the ghost, and now he wasn't there when Nutty needed him.

It took another couple of minutes, without another sound, before Nutty got up the courage, but he knew he had to walk down that hallway and check the bedrooms. He couldn't relax until he did.

And so Nutty got up from his chair and told his legs to move. He even decided to walk quickly and loudly and scare the thing off, if it was down there. But his legs wouldn't listen to his head, and Nutty ended up walking slowly and quietly.

He switched the light on in the hallway, which was getting dark by now. Nothing was there. And so Nutty made his feet take one step after another until he reached the point where his and his sister's bedroom doors were opposite each other.

Chances were his own bedroom was the more

likely spot. He opened the door, slowly, but then he stepped back a little. "I'm coming in," he tried to yell, but sort of whispered. "Clear out or I'll call the cops."

He wanted to reach in and flip the lights on, but he imagined a hand shooting out and grabbing his wrist.

So Nutty stood there, waiting, trying to get up the nerve. "I'm coming in," he said again, even softer. "I know Tae Kwon Do," he lied.

And suddenly he reached in and slapped at the wall until he found the switch. But he jumped back at the same time, and he found that he was out of breath.

Maybe he should go and call William.

Or break and run.

No. He could handle this. He didn't want William coming in and taking over.

He couldn't hear a thing. Maybe that first sound was just something outside . . . or . . . something . . .

He reached out and swung the door open wider and looked in.

Nothing.

Just his bedroom, looking normal—very messy, but empty.

And so Nutty stepped in. He looked all around, especially behind the door, and he felt much better. Then he walked to the closet and opened the door.

And screamed!

The scream came out of him before he even knew what he had seen. He went spinning away, stumbling, scrambling. Then he heard the voice.

"Stop!" was all it said.

Nutty was on the floor, rolling up like a potato bug. There was no use running. The guy—the skinny guy in the weird clothes—was standing in the closet doorway, looking down at him.

"I warned you. Didn't you believe me?"

"Yeah!" Nutty blurted out, but he couldn't have put enough words together to attempt an excuse.

"You didn't believe me," the man said, slowly and deeply, and then he moaned, sounding weary and angry. He was not some glimmering light now. He was the whole man, exactly as he had looked on the street. "I warned you and you wouldn't believe me. But the wall came down."

"Okay. Okay. I won't go over there anymore. Honest."

The man—the ghost—nodded slowly, and was about to speak again. Then a light flashed.

At that same instant, the figure vanished.

Nutty was still wrapped up with his own knees, unable to get himself to do anything. He was breathing hard, clinging to himself, hoping that this was the last of all this—ghosts, movies, bad lines, kisses, everything.

And then a voice spoke from behind him.

Nutty did a sort of rolling leap and crashed against the opposite wall by the closet door. He threw his hands out, warding off whatever might come. But slowly the words were sinking in.

"Nutty, don't be startled," he had heard, and now the source of the voice was poking its head out from under Nutty's bed. "I'm coming out now," the head said.

It was William, of course. Nutty had known the voice from the beginning, but he hadn't been able to tell his body not to react.

"William, what are you doing, trying to kill me?"

"I'm sorry. I didn't know how to let you know I was under there without scaring you."

And now Nutty saw that William was holding a camera, a Polaroid. He even remembered the little buzzing sound after the flash of light, and he could see that the picture was hanging out of the front of the camera.

He knew, suddenly, what had happened. William had taken a picture of the ghost. That was the flash.

But the whole idea was infuriating. Right while

70

Nutty had been taking leave of his senses on the floor, William had been snapping pictures.

William pulled himself out from under the bed and then sat up and leaned back. He detached the film and watched for the picture to appear. "Nutty, this could be big. I just hope I got him."

"William, you are the most . . . how can you even think that I would . . ." But Nutty couldn't come up with the right words to express his outrage.

"Look, I know. It was frightening. And maybe I should have taken the picture a little sooner. But I felt like we needed to hear what he had to say. And besides, I've got a recorder running down here. I wanted to get him on tape, if I could."

"William, that guy is going to get me one of these times. Probably rip my head off or something. And all you're worried about is snapping off a good picture."

"No, no . . . ." But William's attention was on the picture. "Well," he finally said, "no luck there." He turned the film around and showed Nutty. The picture was blank, totally white. "Either I had the camera set wrong, or the stuff people say is true about not being able to take a picture of a ghost."

Nutty had finally flattened out on the floor. He was trying to get his breath. "William, I don't care.

I don't need a picture of the guy. I've seen him plenty. What I want to do is get rid of him."

William didn't comment. He was reaching under the bed, with his plump little fanny sticking up in the air. And then he withdrew his head from under the bed, sat up, and turned around again. He punched the rewind button, and while the cassette tape made a whirring sound, he said, absently, "Sure, Nutty. If I at least got his voice, I think we can . . ."

The tape clicked as it reached the end, and William pushed the PLAY button and then waited. A long silence followed during which Nutty tried to think what he could do. He knew he was going to quit the movie, but how was he going to convince his parents—and everyone else—that he had no choice?

He heard a distant voice saying, "I'm coming in." And then, "Clear out or I'll call the cops."

"Good idea, Nutty," William said, and he chuckled. "Call the cops on a ghost? Did you think they could catch him in a butterfly net or something?"

"Lay off, William."

"I'm coming in," the recorded voice said again. "I know Tae Kwon Do."

William really laughed at that one. "Oh, Nutty," he said. "You're a tiger."

"Eat my gym socks, William! There's a nice dirty pair over there in the corner."

Nutty felt like a real jerk. Tae Kwon Do on a ghost? He didn't really know Tae Kwon Do anyway. And the ghost knew that besides. There was no winning this game.

A long silence was hissing from the recorder, followed by a scream and a crashing noise—Nutty's dive onto the floor—and then, after a time, Nutty's voice blurting out, "Yeah!"

"Nothing," William said, but he kept listening.

"Okay. Okay. I won't go over there anymore. Honest," Nutty heard himself say on the recorder, and William punched the button.

"Nothing at all," William said. "We got you—but not him. That's really discouraging. I thought we had it."

"How did you get in here anyway?" Nutty suddenly thought to ask.

"I know where you keep your key on the porch. I let myself in. I hope you don't mind."

"I do."

"Nutty, it was the perfect chance. I couldn't miss it. I was almost sure, after today, that he would come back again tonight. I figured if I was ready with my camera and my recorder, I could get him."

"Why didn't you tell me? You didn't have to break into my house, for crying out loud."

"Well, I was a little concerned about your knowing. For all I know, a ghost can tune in on thoughts." But William's mind was elsewhere. He looked discouraged. "If I can't get a picture of him, or get him on tape, I don't know what I can do. I'm really disappointed about this."

"William, never mind. What you gotta do is get me out of that movie. You're my agent."

"Hey, I can't do that."

"I don't care about the money or . . . anything. I'm out. And that's it."

"No way, Nutty. You can't do that."

"Why not?"

"Because we'll never prove the existence of that ghost if you stop giving him a reason to show up."

Nutty couldn't speak. There were no words to express what he wanted to say. And so finally he just blurted out, "Get out of here!"

"Oh, thanks a lot," William said. "I go to all this trouble and then you tell me to get out?"

That was enough for Nutty. He stood up and walked over to William. "Get out. I don't ever want to see you again."

"What are you talking about, Nutty?"

"You don't care about me. You're not a friend. You never have been."

"Come on, Nutty. You're just angry. You're being completely irrational."

74

"William, you'll do anything to get what you want. People don't mean anything to you. You always tell me that you're changing, but I don't see it. So just get away from me. I'll handle things for myself from now on."

"Nutty, I don't think you're in danger. I keep telling you that. And now I have some proof. I did some checking this afternoon, and I found out that Matthew Graham was an important actor. He died two years ago. It could be the same man. The costume you described sounds like the sort of thing you see in a Shakespeare play, and Matthew Graham was famous for his Shakespearean performances."

"William, what does that have to do with anything?"

"I'm not entirely sure. But if he was a great actor, you could see why he might not be able to rest in his grave with this sort of film being made."

"Or he might want to get *me* because my acting won't let him sleep."

"Well, true. But I still say that if he wanted to hurt you, he's had plenty of chances. I think he just wants to scare you away."

"Well, fine. You think that all you want. But do your thinking somewhere else. Not in my house. And don't look for me at the set in the morning."

"Okay, fine," William said. "But don't call me

when things start going badly for you. I won't be around to get you out of this mess—the way I always have before." He collected his camera and recorder, and he left.

Nutty sat down on his bed and took a deep breath. He was glad to get rid of William.

He was on his own now—and scared—but he liked it better that way.

Chapter 7

*N*utty had his mind made up. He spent some time that night thinking what he wanted to say to his parents. And when they got home, he asked them to sit down with him in the living room, and he gave his little speech.

"Mom and Dad, I know you want me to be a movie star and make a lot of money and stuff, but I'm a terrible actor."

At that point, his dad tried to break in, but Nutty said, "Just listen to me for a minute, okay?" His dad agreed and sat back in his big chair. But he didn't look pleased.

"I can't act at all. And I've tried hard. Part of the problem is that Mr. Deveraux is the worst director in the world, and he makes me overdo everything. I'm not kidding, if this movie ever came out, it would make you sick. It would make that little part I did on TV look great by comparison."

"Really?" Mom asked, and she made a face, as though she had just smelled something disgusting.

"Yeah. I'm serious. It's that bad," Nutty told her. "But that's not the only thing. There's something else going on that's really weird. I know you'll think I'm making this up, but I'm not."

And then he told them the whole story about the ghost, the visits in his room, the things happening on the set, and William's attempt to photograph the guy. By the time he was finished, Mom looked scared, and Dad looked really skeptical.

"Oh, come on, Freddie," Dad said. "Do you expect us to believe something like that?"

"No, I guess I don't. But it's true. Every word of it."

Dad slipped down in his chair and let his long legs slide way out in front of him. For a time, he put the tips of his fingers together and stared at them. Nutty knew he was thinking everything over. Mom, in the meantime, was asking lots of questions—about every detail of what had happened.

Finally Dad said, "Look, Freddie, I don't believe in ghosts. There must be some logical explanation for all this. What I suspect is that a man, for some reason, is trying to scare you out of continuing to do this movie."

"Dad, he glowed in the dark."

"Well, that could be a trick of some sort."

"And how did he disappear? When William's camera flashed—*poof*—he was gone."

"Or did he hurry to the door and run out?"

"No way. He just . . . vanished."

"Fred, this scares me," Mom said. "I think Freddie's in real danger."

"If the guy had wanted to hurt Freddie, he could have done it anytime he wanted to," Dad answered.

"That's what William says."

"Well, William's a very smart boy." Dad sat up straight. "I know he can be annoying, but he's a thinker. Maybe he's got this pegged. Why give in to these scare tactics? Why don't we just call the police? They could watch the house at night and patrol the set during the filming."

Nutty couldn't believe this. It was like dealing with William all over again. He stood up. "Dad, the guy has never been seen on the set. But things keep going wrong, and yesterday some people could have been hurt."

"Come on, Freddie, I'm sure things always go wrong on a movie set."

But Nutty had listened to enough of this.

"Dad, I'm *not* going to finish the movie," he said, and he meant it. Then he walked back to his bedroom.

What followed was a very long night. Nutty didn't sleep well, and every little sound seemed like a crash in his ears. He kept the door open and the hall light on, but that only made things worse. When he would awaken, the light, for a moment, would seem like a figure standing near his bed, and every time, he was startled.

Eventually, however, he did fall into a deep sleep. When morning came, he was finally resting well. That's when he heard the doorbell ring— once, and then, rather quickly, a second time. He was gradually waking, and he wondered who would be at his house so early.

He heard someone go to the door and open it, and then he heard his dad say, "Yes, officer, it is."

Officer?

"Yes. Just a minute. I'll get him," Dad said, and he sounded concerned.

Nutty got up and grabbed his old terry cloth robe. He was already at his bedroom door when his dad got there. "Freddie, two policemen are out here. They want to talk to you."

So Nutty tramped down the hallway to the living room, where the policemen were standing. One of them was an older man with a gray mustache and graying hair around his ears. He was holding his hat in his hands and was standing with his legs spread wide. He didn't look very cheery.

"Good morning," the man said, in a raspy voice. And then he looked at a notepad and asked, "What's the deal on your name, son? Is it Parker House or Frederick Nutsell?"

Dad answered before Nutty could. "It's both, sir. Parker House is his stage name."

"But his real name is Frederick, right?"

"Yes," Mr. Nutsell said. He laughed nervously. "But we call him Freddie, and the kids all call him Nutty."

The man didn't smile. Neither did his partner. He was a neat-looking young man, except that he had a rather heavy growth of whiskers, as though he hadn't had a chance to shave yet that morning.

Now Mom was coming down the hallway. "What's wrong?" she said, sleepily.

"We need to ask your son some questions," the older man answered.

"Sit down," Mom said.

But the policeman said, "This is fine." And then he looked down at Nutty. "Where were you during the night—around one to one-thirty in the morning?"

Nutty was relieved. That was an easy one to answer. "In bed. Right down there."

"You didn't leave during the night?"

"No."

And Dad added, "He went to bed quite early, actually. He was here all night."

"Do you have any way to prove that he didn't leave during the night?"

"Well, no. But he never does. I mean, where would he go?"

The officer looked at Nutty again. "Did you leave the house last night and go over to the school? To the movie set?"

"No." Nutty didn't like this. How could he prove that he hadn't left his bed all night?

"I'm afraid we have witnesses who say otherwise. Some vandalism was done to the set last night, and a security officer identified you as the perpetrator. He said he chased you, but you managed to get away from him."

Now Nutty knew. But what was he supposed to tell this policeman—that a ghost was going around taking on his form?

"It wasn't me," Nutty said. "I was never over there."

"Officer," Mr. Nutsell said, "Freddie is the star of that movie. Why would he want to damage the set?"

"I don't know. But I have an eyewitness who has no doubt whatsoever that your son was the one who did it."

Nutty could see that his dad was adding up

what he knew. Nutty had vowed not to be in the movie and then had gone to bed. He could have easily slipped out of the house, and the walk to the school was only ten minutes or so. Mr. Nutsell took a good, hard look at Nutty. "Freddie, did you do this?" he asked.

"Dad, *no*," Nutty said, and he looked his father clearly in the eyes. "But now do you believe me about the other stuff I told you?"

Dad considered.

The officer said, "What's this about 'other stuff'? Are you saying you know who might have done it?"

"Yeah, I know, but you won't believe me."

"Just tell me what you know," the man said, and his voice had never once changed from the same steady, tired tone.

Nutty glanced at his parents. Dad had his arm around his wife's waist, and they were both looking worried. "A ghost has been—"

But his dad suddenly said, "Actually, that's only one theory. Freddie has this idea about a . . . well, here's what I think. Some fellow is trying to disrupt the movie, and he's been harassing Freddie. He's even come into our house."

"What guy?"

"Tell the officer what the man looks like, Freddie."

Nutty knew this was useless but he said, "He's

tall and skinny, and he wears old-fashioned clothes. Puffy, short pants and long stockings. He's got this real low voice, and he talks like he's from England."

"And this man came into your house?"

Nutty could see that the policeman was having a hard enough time buying this. How was he supposed believe that the thing could "appear" whenever it wanted to? "It's a long story," Nutty said. "But I was not over at the set last night. Honest. I promise you I wasn't."

The officer's look never changed. His eyes hardly seemed to focus on anything. He merely said, "Well, the person seen last night was a kid, not some tall, skinny man. And the kid was you, according to our witness. That's what I've got to go on. I think we better all go down to the police station, and we'll have to take a formal statement. Son, I hope you know that vandalism is very serious business."

"Of course, he knows that," Mom said. "Freddie's never done anything like that."

"Well, ma'am, I don't know about that. We'll just have to look into this whole thing a little deeper. If you don't mind, we'll just drive over . . ."

But just then the doorbell rang again.

Dad stepped into the nearby entrance and opened the door. Nutty heard Mr. Deveraux say, loudly, "Are the police already here?" And then he burst into the house, pushing past Dad as though he were some mere obstacle in his way.

"Officers, there's been a tragic mistake," he said, and he waved his arms as though he were signalling time out in a football game. "This boy is not the vandal. I've spoken with our security officer, and he now tells me that he was mistaken."

"But, sir, I talked to him not an hour ago, and he said he had no doubt—"

"Yes, yes. He told me that. But the more he thought about it, the more he realized that Parker House, our leading man, would never do such a thing. He said it could have been that Orlando boy—the one with the small part. What's his name, Parker?"

"Orlando wouldn't do anything like that," Nutty said.

"Sure he would," Mr. Deveraux almost shouted. "The kid's angry about not getting a bigger part. It would be just like him to take out his anger that way. In fact, the more I think about it, I'm almost sure he's the one."

"What's the boy's name?" the officer asked again.

"Orlando Ortega," Mr. Nutsell said, "but I can vouch for him too. He's not that kind of boy."

"You don't know *that*!" Deveraux said, his eyes

looking wild. "You can't trust anyone these days. Everyone's out to get me, I swear." Then he seemed to think about what he had said. "But I know it was not Parker here. We press no charges. We want the whole thing dropped."

"What about this other boy?"

"Oh. Well, no. Not him either. Let's just forget the whole thing. Boys will be boys, you know."

"Sir, this was vandalism."

"Well, yes, but the damage was not that great. Let's drop the whole thing. I'll talk to Orlando, take him under my arm, guide him to better things. It's the least I can do. These young actors are like my own children." He wrapped his short little arm around Nutty and gave him a solid squeeze.

The officer shook his head. "We got up awful early in the morning for this," he said to his partner, and the young man nodded, looking disgusted. The two policemen left.

Deveraux walked with them to the door, apologizing all the way for the "terrible mistake."

As soon as the door was shut, Deveraux spun around. "Now, young man," he pronounced in a loud voice, and he pointed a finger at Nutty, "answer to me. Why did you want to rip up my set? Just tell me. Haven't I treated you like a son? Haven't I made you a star?"

Deveraux moved in on Nutty, stabbing with his finger, and Nutty stepped back. "Wait just a

86

minute," Dad was saying, and he grabbed Deveraux's shoulder. "What are you talking about? Freddie was here all night."

Deveraux spun around. "Who in the world is Freddie?"

"Nutty. I mean, Parker."

"You mean this gutter rat? You mean this scummy brat? This enemy who stabbed me in the back after I gave him the chance of a lifetime?"

But Mom had heard about enough of that. "What are you talking about?" she demanded. "You just told the police he didn't do it."

"Yes. That's what I told *them*. I can't have my star in some juvenile lockup, can I? We start filming in . . ." Deveraux looked at his watch. "In an hour. These things happen. It may have been nervous exhaustion, or sleepwalking. I don't know. Just get dressed. I'll wait. We need to get rolling."

Nutty took a long breath. "Mr. Deveraux, I'm quitting the movie," Nutty said.

"So! You are a traitor. I knew it, you slimy little slug. But you won't get away with this. All I have to do is call those officers back and you're history, my friend. You're in the slammer!"

"Mr. Deveraux, there's something going on. Someone wants to stop the movie. He's warned me to stay away from the set. And besides, I can't act, and you know it."

"I knew it. I knew I had enemies. They're

trying to get me. They're always trying to get me. They're everywhere." He ran his fingers through his hair so wildly that Nutty was surprised he didn't pull his toupee loose.

Nutty tried to calm the man down by asking, softly, "Couldn't you find someone else to finish the movie?"

"Not a chance. We're three weeks behind schedule now, and we've only been filming *two* weeks. Explain that one. Tell me I don't have enemies."

Nutty didn't try. "Sir, all I know is that I want out of the whole thing. This is the worst experience I've ever had."

"Of course it is, son. Oh, you lovely kid, don't you know? Art is like that. It hurts. The only joy comes after the pain. So put on your shoes, and let's go. Let's make the best film this world has ever seen, and then let's share the joy. But for now, let's go back and face the pain."

"No. I'm just not going to—"

"I said, get your shoes on, worm rot. I'll sue you for everything you've got, and everything this imbecile of a father ever hopes to make. I'll throw you in jail, sue you for breach of contract, trump up anything I can against your parents, and never stop until I drive your whole family into poverty. Do you understand that?"

"Son," Dad said, "I don't think we have any choice. You have a contract. You'll have to finish the film."

Deveraux spun to Mr. Nutsell. "Sir, you're a gentleman. I admire you and respect you. And I'll give Parker a five-thousand-dollar bonus to thank you—*if* we get this film finished." He stuck out his hand.

Nutty couldn't believe it. Dad nodded his head in agreement and stuck out his own hand to shake on the deal.

Nutty gave up.

What could he do?

He went to look for his shoes.

Chapter 8

*N*utty went off with Mr. Deveraux in the limousine, and all the way to the set the man talked. He talked about his enemies; he called Parker ungrateful; he apologized and hugged Nutty and told him he knew what stress could do. And when Nutty said he wasn't the vandal, he said, "Good, son. Stick with that story. I'll say the same thing. But if you try it again, I'll rip your nose hairs out, one at a time. Do you understand that?"

Nutty didn't. Nutty didn't understand anything anymore. The world was crazy.

The next crazy thing that happened was that Nutty's "former friend" William was waiting when Nutty arrived, and he said, "Nutty, I've got to talk to you."

"I've got to get my makeup on," Nutty said, but he really meant, "I don't want to talk."

90

"Just give me two minutes," William said.

So Nutty stepped aside with him even though Mr. Deveraux was screaming for him to get to the makeup trailer.

"Look, Nutty," William said, "I thought a lot about what you said last night. I'm afraid you're right—at least in part. I do get carried away sometimes and—"

"William, don't give me another one of your phony apologies. All you want to do is calm me down. Then you'll be right back to your old tricks."

"No, really, Nutty. I know I take advantage of people sometimes. It's hard not to use my superior . . . uh—"

"Yeah, that's it, William. You think you're so smart that you can get me to do anything you want."

"Well, all right. I guess that is what I do at times. But I don't exactly mean to."

"It doesn't matter, William. I'm just not going to let you make my decisions anymore."

"Good. That's the way I want it."

"William, you've said stuff like that before. Then, the next thing I know, you've talked me into something again."

"Not really. I just—"

"William, you do."

"Well, okay. I guess I do. But I'll try not to. And if you see me doing it, just tell me."

Nutty blew out a long breath. "Yeah, right," he said. He still didn't trust William.

"Nutty, why are you here this morning anyway? I thought you were quitting."

Deveraux had disappeared for a minute, but now he was back and screaming, "Parker, get to that trailer now or I'll find another actor to . . . well, no. But please hurry."

"I can't quit," Nutty said to William.

He walked off to the makeup trailer with William tagging along. And William kept asking questions until he got the whole story.

Then, while the makeup woman dabbed away at Nutty, William sat and thought. When they finally stepped down from the trailer, William said, "Do you want to know what I think?"

"No, as a matter of fact, I don't."

"Well, fine."

Nutty kept walking.

"I just thought you might like to have my opinion. You would still make the decision, of course."

"William, you're going to tell me one way or the other. So go ahead."

"No, that's all right."

"William! Out with it."

"Well, all right." But now he thought for a moment. "Here's how I see it. You want out of the movie, and you're being blackmailed by Deveraux. Right?"

Nutty nodded.

"Are you really sure you wouldn't be sorry if you were out of the film, and you lost all the money and all the attention?"

"Who wants attention for being *bad* at something?"

"What about the money?"

"I'd rather make money doing something I'm good at."

"Okay. Here's what I'm thinking. Maybe we need to work with the ghost, not against him."

"What do you mean 'we,' William?"

"Okay. You."

"So what's your point? How could I work with the ghost?"

"I'm not exactly sure. I just think you both want the same thing—the end of the movie. There ought to be a way to cooperate with each other."

"Yeah, I can start bonking people over the head and knocking them down."

"Well, no. But maybe—"

"No, William. I'm not interested."

Nutty and William had reached the set, but as usual, the crew was having some problems. The shoot couldn't begin yet.

"I do wish the ghost knew that I wanted out," Nutty said. "Maybe he would lay off me then."

"Now that's an idea, Nutty. If we could talk to him, maybe we could work something out."

"No way. I don't want the guy to show up in my bedroom again."

"Well, maybe we could meet him on his own turf. We could go look for him."

"Oh, sure."

"It might be possible. I have a theory about where he's been hanging out."

"William, you're doing it again. You have a plan, and you're acting like you don't. You know exactly what you want me to do."

William stuck his hands in his pockets and looked down at the grass. "Uh . . . well . . . actually that *is* true," he said. "I'm sorry to admit it, but you're exactly right. It's not an easy habit to give up."

And he walked away.

Nutty was taken by surprise. But he also knew this could be another one of William's tricks. He wasn't going to chase after him.

Besides, Deveraux was suddenly screaming for his actors to get on the set. It was time to refilm the "buddy" scene—if the rebuilt wall would work.

Nutty walked to the set, but he watched the wall. He was going to be very careful today.

Near the set, a lot of kids he knew were hanging around—the same as they did every day. Some were from the lab school, and some were from other schools in town.

"Good morning," one of the girls said, with a musical ring. "Good luck today. We're all cheering for you, Parker."

"Hey, Patty, don't call me Parker," Nutty said.

"We think 'Parker' fits you," a girl named Nicole said.

A kid named Justin, a sixth-grader from the lab school, said, "A hotshot movie star can't be named Nutty."

"Or Frederick," Patty said.

"Hey, you guys, just because I'm in a movie, that doesn't mean I'm a different person. I—"

"But you *are*," Nicole said.

Nutty gave up. He turned to walk away, but one of the other girls, a fourth-grader named Christina said, "Parker, can I get your autograph for my cousin?"

"Christina, no. I'm not going to start signing autographs. That's just stupid."

"Oh, pleeeease."

"I'll tell you what. I'll sign Orlando Ortega. He's going to be a big star." Nutty had spotted Orlando walking from the trailer toward the set.

"That's right," Orlando said. "I'm going for the big time." He smiled and ran his hand across his hair one more time—something he did about twice a minute now.

"You're not a star," Nicole whined.

"Hey," Nutty said, "he's getting an agent, and

he's going for it. And I'm quitting as soon as this movie is finished. Besides, he's better looking than I am. He told me so."

"You got that right," Orlando said. "Every time I look in a mirror, I say, 'Tom Cruise, eat your heart out.' "

"Actually, you look more like another movie star," Nutty said. "That one you see in the TV reruns all the time."

"Who?"

"I can't think of the name. But your nose, your hair. Everything is just the same."

"Who?"

"Oh, yeah. It's coming to me. It's an actor named Lassie."

"Cute, Nutty. Really cute."

Nutty turned to the group of kids. "Orlando really is headed for the top. He told me. You better get his autograph."

No one seemed interested.

"Really," Nutty said. "He's handsome. He's a good actor. This first part is just the beginning. And me, I'm quitting. So I won't be anything to your cousin."

Several seconds passed, and then Christina reached out with her slip of paper. "Well, okay. I might as well get it. Just in case."

Nutty laughed as he walked to the set.

But the wall was not holding together just

right, and the shoot would be delayed a few more minutes. What else was new?

Nutty saw Sarah sitting on the grass. He walked over and sat down next to her. She looked nice this morning in a pair of shorts and a pink shirt. Anything was better than that country-girl outfit she had to wear most of the time.

"How come you came over so early?" Nutty asked. "We probably won't have this scene finished for hours."

"I know. I couldn't sleep this morning, so I just got up and came over."

"How come you couldn't sleep?"

"I don't know. I've got a lot on my mind."

"Like what?"

She looked Nutty over, as though she weren't sure that he really wanted to know. But then she said, quietly, "I hate making this movie. I don't like being screamed at, and I don't like missing my whole summer. And I don't like the way my friends are treating me."

"What are they doing?" Nutty asked.

"Mindy is telling everyone I'm stuck-up—just because she got a small part in the movie and I got a big one. And my friends who aren't in the movie are all jealous. They don't even talk to me anymore. And it's all because of this stupid movie."

"Do you really think it's stupid?"

"Don't you?"

"Yeah. It's more than stupid. It's like . . . stupendously stupid."

Sarah laughed. "My dad watched one day, and he said it was 'ludicrous.' I don't know what that means. But it sounds like a pretty good word for it."

"Don't you want to be famous?" Nutty asked.

"No. Not for making a ludicrous movie."

"What if it was a good one?" Nutty asked, seriously.

Sarah thought it over. "I still don't like it. I just want my old life back—and everyone treating me regular again. I'd quit right now if I could."

"Yeah, me too. But look at Orlando," Nutty said. "He's over there signing autographs. I just made him famous, and it only took about a minute."

Sarah laughed. "Yeah, that's about how real this star stuff is."

"It's stupid," Nutty said.

"Ludicrous," Sarah added, and they both laughed.

But Nutty also had another thought.

What if the ghost hurt someone—someone like Sarah? Maybe it would be better to be locked up for vandalism than to let that happen. He wondered whether he was doing the right thing.

"Sarah," he said. "Be really careful today. Okay?"

"Why?"

"Uh . . . I don't know. Some bad things have happened around here—like that wall falling down. So watch out, okay?"

"Okay," she said. "Thanks." She smiled just a little. "Do you know what scene we're doing after you guys finish this one?" she asked.

"No. What?"

"You do the one with your buddies, and then you do the fight over—the one where you hit that guy before. And then we do the one where I tell you that you're my hero and everything."

"Oh, no. That's the one where I . . ."

"Yup. That's the other time you kiss me."

"Oh, man. That makes me sick."

Sarah laughed. "I know," she said.

"I don't mean . . . you know . . ."

"Hey, I know what you're talking about. That last time was the worst."

"I thought kissing was supposed to be exciting or something. But that was just sort of . . . blah."

Sarah laughed. "I know. It was about as exciting as licking a stamp." But then she said, "Oh, I didn't mean . . . well, you know . . ."

But Nutty knew exactly what she meant. They both laughed for a long time.

It was strange.

Now that they didn't want to kiss each other anymore, Nutty thought he liked her more than ever.

99

Chapter 9

inally, the set was ready, and Deveraux got all the "buddies" out in front of the wall. He had people behind it, holding on, and ropes tied to it, just in case. And the thing held together. But the scene didn't. Or at least it was just as bad as ever. Nutty finally choked out all his love for his buddies, and Orlando delivered his great line:

"Gee, Hank, you're the best friend I've ever had. I *value* our relationship."

Twenty takes, at least.

Orlando couldn't make the line sound honest, no matter how much Deveraux praised or hated him. And in the end, Deveraux said "print" because he gave up. Nutty was sure of that. If anything, Orlando was getting worse, the harder he tried.

In any case, Nutty's buddies finally moved off the set, and the Hell's Cherubs moved in. Nutty had to run through the fight scene with them a few times before the shoot would begin. And Deveraux was angry that Nutty had "forgotten" everything.

But this was the first time through for Nutty. The time before the ghost had played the role and socked the socks off one of the biggest men Nutty had ever seen. He didn't think there would be much danger of that today.

The whole idea was nuts to Nutty anyway. He took on eight giant guys who had chains and clubs. They were all big guys, and Nutty had to flip them around with all his Tae Kwon Do moves. The only trouble was, the Tae Kwon Do expert who was supposed to be Nutty's advisor had somehow never made it to Warrensburg. Nutty had to do whatever Deveraux imagined was a Tae Kwon Do technique. Usually that meant grabbing these big guys' fists out of the air and then stepping under their arms and flipping them over on their backs.

Deveraux taught Nutty a couple of chops too—karate, or whatever. A quick blow with his knuckles would render these guys unconscious for the rest of the scene—or as long as they weren't needed to keep the fight going on endlessly.

But it was all choreographed, with one or two

coming at Nutty at a time. All eight never jumped him at once. That was too logical. So Nutty took them on as they came at him, and each time, he made short work of them. *Blam*, down they would drop, like lumps of bread dough, and Nutty would spin around and face the next one—or two.

And then it happened.

About the third time through the practice, Nutty shot out one of his usual knuckle shots to a big guy's chest—except that he pulled the punch back about six inches short of hitting the guy. The actor was supposed to fall backwards. But this guy didn't just fall.

He flew.

He was sent spinning through the air, as if someone had picked him up and tossed him. As he crashed on the ground with a huge thud, Nutty heard the wind blow out of the man, and he heard him moan. He could see the guy couldn't get up.

"Wonderful, Stanley, wonderful," Deveraux called out. He turned around and looked at the others. "Mario, Peter, that's just exactly what I want you to do. Really give it a ride. Sail through the air like that, and then give it that crushing sound, and the big exhale, just the way Stanley did."

But by now Mario was saying, "What are you talking about? That was no stunt."

A cameraman—a guy everyone called O. C.—

kneeled down by Stanley. "He's unconscious," he said. "He hit the ground hard."

Nutty ran to Stanley. He heard someone behind him say, "The kid must have really caught him. Did you see that guy flip in the air?"

But Deveraux was saying, "Oh, no. Stanley's just giving us a little entertainment here. What a kidder. Come on, get up, you crazy son of a gun." He waited maybe three seconds, and then he shouted, "I said, get up, eggs-for-brains. We've got work to do."

Finally Stanley did begin to stir. His eyes opened slowly and he looked around and blinked. "Where am I?" he said.

"What an actor!" Deveraux shouted. "What a goof. I love you, Stanley. You're too much."

But poor Stanley was still coming out with bad lines. "How long have I been like this?" he asked. Maybe poor Stanley had played too many bad movies—Deveraux movies.

Nutty thought Stanley was all right. But he knew how badly he could have been hurt. He could have broken his neck falling like that. Nutty was making up his mind. Enough was enough.

"Mr. Deveraux, he's not faking," Nutty said. "I know what happened to him."

But William hurried up next to Nutty and said, "Yeah, Parker accidentally hit him, and he got in a perfect shot and just happened to knock him—"

"William, shut up," Nutty said. "That's not true."

But William whispered fiercely, "Don't tell him. Let's try to talk to the ghost first."

"No, William." Nutty stepped away. "Mr. Deveraux, a ghost is trying to ruin the movie. I've seen him. He's talked to me, and he warned me to quit filming or he'll . . . do something to me."

Deveraux had his hands on his hips. He was shaking his head slowly back and forth. "Oh, Parker, Parker—why are you actors all so high-strung and imaginative? I don't know why I put up with you."

"Well, you don't have to anymore. I'm quitting the film. You can sue, or you can have me put in jail, or anything else you want to do. But I'm not going to be in your movie. This ghost guy just isn't going to stop until he ruins everything."

"I swear, half the actors I know are absolutely insane," Deveraux said. He tossed his clipboard on the ground. "I thought I could come out here to Hicktown, USA, and I could find myself some normal, regular kids, and make a *real* movie about *real* people. But no such luck. I've got myself another lunatic." He looked around at the crew. "No wonder kids around here call the boy 'Nutty.' "

But Stanley was getting up now, and he said,

"Sir, the kid never hit me. The punch was short, just like it was supposed to be. Something picked me up and tossed me."

"Put them in the same cell!" Deveraux screamed. "A padded cell. That's where these two belong."

But one of the other Hell's Cherubs, a huge guy named Seth, was holding onto Stanley, helping him keep his balance. "I gotta say, some awfully strange things are happening around here. I've never seen this much stuff happen on one set."

"Enemies. That's why," Deveraux moaned. "I always have enemies. I'm too brilliant and creative for my own good. Everyone is out to get me."

"Well, anyway," Nutty said, "I'm going now. Sorry this didn't work out. But look at it this way, it was an awful movie. It would have been bad for everyone to have it come out in the theaters."

"What?" Deveraux chased after Nutty, who was now walking fast. "What? What did you say? I'll sue you for talking that way about my picture. You can't get away with that."

"So sue me," Nutty said, and he left. But he didn't get far before William came running after him.

"Nutty, wait. Wait," he was yelling. "Think about this before you decide."

Nutty didn't turn around, but when William caught up, he said, "I've already thought about it."

"Well, think some more. Do you really want to get arrested and sued? The guy will do it."

"William, leave me alone. I'm making up my own mind about this." But inside, Nutty was churning. He had gotten awfully used to William making decisions like this. And facing juvenile court for vandalism—not to mention an angry father—was hardly anything to get excited about.

He also knew what else was hard to face. "William, that ghost is getting meaner all the time. What if he works me over one of these days? Or hurts one of you guys? Or Sarah? I can't defend myself against a guy like that. He can do anything he wants."

"Okay. I know that. But that's why we need to talk to him."

"What good is that going to do?"

"Maybe none. But it's worth a try."

"William, you're trying to tell me what to do again."

"Not exactly. I'm just worried what might happen to you. I'm trying to think what we can do to keep you from getting in a bigger mess."

"Yeah, right."

"No, really. This is not some trick this time to get pictures of him—or anything like that."

Nutty was still walking. "So where would we find him?"

"I don't know for sure. But I've got an idea where to look."

"And where's that?" Nutty was trying to sound uninterested.

"Okay. I had a librarian friend of mine at the university do some checking on this Matthew Graham. I called the library this morning, and my friend had come up with some interesting stuff. Graham spent most of his life acting on the stage. But at the end of his career, he did a couple of movies."

"I don't see how that—"

"Just listen to me. I guess he needed the money, and he took anything he could get. But the very last movie he did was . . . are you ready for this?"

"Just tell me, William."

"It was called *Golden Moonset*, and guess who the director was?"

Nutty shrugged, but then it hit him. Only one man would direct a movie with a name that stupid. "Deveraux?" he said, and William nodded. That *was* interesting.

"My theory is," William said, "the guy was humiliated to be in such a bad movie. It got horrible reviews. Maybe he can't forgive himself for stooping so low—or something like that. It all fits. He's out to ruin the movie, or maybe Deveraux himself. He can't rest in his grave until he gets the job done."

It all sounded like a plot to another bad movie—one Deveraux could direct himself. And yet the coincidence was pretty amazing. "So I still don't get the point," Nutty said. "Where do you think we would find him?"

"Here's what makes sense to me. He might be hanging out in the theater on campus. Backstage, or somewhere like that. Wouldn't that be where an actor would want to be if he were in this town?"

"Maybe. I've never met a lot of ghost actors before."

"Well, it's worth a try. And besides, if he isn't there, he might be following us anyway. He might even be listening to us right now. If he knows we want to talk to him, and that we don't think much of old Deveraux, he might follow us in there and talk to us."

"William, do you really want to go into a dark theater and try to meet up with a ghost?"

"Actually, it might be very interesting. I'd like to ask him all about—you know—the life of a ghost, and that sort of thing."

"See, you're still trying to prove something."

"Well, sure. But I'm thinking about you first—primarily. Honest, Nutty. I am."

Nutty wasn't sure. But he also knew he was almost as afraid of telling his dad what he had done

108

as he was of the ghost. What did he have to lose?

Or perhaps that wasn't the best question to ask. The answer could turn out to be more than he really wanted to deal with right now.

Still, he said, "Okay. I guess we can try. But you do the talking. I don't think I can manage it."

"No problem. I've never been speechless in my whole life."

Nutty knew that was true. "But you can't make any deals I don't agree with."

"Of course not."

The two nodded, and then they turned back toward campus. But as they did, Nutty felt a strange fear come over him, and he shuddered. He had a feeling that William was right. The ghost would be waiting for them.

And that thought was almost more than he could face. He remembered how he had felt when the thing had been in his room. Maybe he would be better off to go to jail.

But something also told him that it was time to do things right, that he had to get things straightened out. "William," he said. "I'm serious about one thing. I won't make any deals that just keep this whole mess going."

"Fine. I agree."

But Nutty wondered whether he could trust William. He knew he had to keep the guy from taking control again.

Chapter 10

*N*utty and William entered the building and then moved slowly down the dark hallway. They walked around the theater toward the backstage doors, but the deeper into the hallway they got, the deeper the darkness.

William found the door to the backstage area, and he slowly opened it. He reached in and felt along the wall, but then he said, "I don't know where the lights are. They're not by the door."

Nutty was not at all excited about stepping into the blackness ahead of them, but when William stepped forward, Nutty went with him.

"Mr. Graham," William said, speaking into the dark. His voice echoed back at them. "Mr. Graham, if you're here somewhere, we want to talk to you. It's William Bilks and Frederick Nutsell—the one you know as Parker House."

The boys stood still and waited.

"We better shut the door," William said.

Nutty didn't like the idea, but William took another step forward, and Nutty wanted to stay close to him. He let go of the door, and it slowly swung shut . . . and clicked. Now all was black.

Nutty could hear someone breathing, slowly, steadily. It had to be William, and yet the sound seemed farther away than that. He could see nothing, and the breathing was the only sound.

And then Nutty felt something—some movement, like the hint of a breeze, warm and stuffy. A strange chill passed through him. He strained to see. And above all, he resisted a desire to spin and run. He remembered how really terrifying it had been to face the presence of that glowing figure in his room. And now William was inviting it back.

"Mr. Graham," William said again, "we wish to speak with you. We know that you were an actor at one time. We know that you made a film with Damian Deveraux, and we think you're trying to stop his current project. We don't blame you for that. We even agree. We're willing to cooperate with you if—"

Nutty gave William a little poke. "No, William," he said. "No cooperation. We're not going to let him knock guys around."

"Okay. Okay," William whispered, but then he spoke loudly again. "Mr. Graham, we think there might be better ways to shut down the movie, and we'd like to talk it over with you. If you are here, please let us know."

The silence was the worst. Nutty waited and stared into the dark. He hated the feeling that something—or someone—could be within reach of him without his even knowing.

Nutty waited a few seconds—though it seemed a few minutes—and then he said, "Okay, William, he's not here. Let's go."

But William hushed him, and then he moved forward again. Nutty stepped ahead too. But when he reached out to find William with his hand, he found nothing. "William, where are you?" he whispered.

But no answer came back. Nutty took another step forward and something brushed against him. He felt the soft heaviness and he spun away. Then he realized he had walked into a backstage curtain. But where was William?

"William. Tell me where you are. Don't leave me."

No answer.

Nutty stood absolutely still. He listened for a footstep, for anything. He only heard a faint whisper or . . . and then he knew that he was hearing the sound of someone breathing again. Steady and deep, like someone sleeping.

"William! Answer me. Where are you?"

Silence.

The breathing was still there. But Nutty couldn't tell where it was coming from.

He no longer knew how to turn and go back. He had lost all sense of direction. He didn't dare move ahead. And so he stood still, frozen, his mind sort of locked on hold. He couldn't think what might have happened to William. The guy had been swallowed up in the darkness and was gone.

"Please, William. I'm scared. Just say something."

Again, nothing.

And then he realized that the breathing was closer. It was coming toward him, moving in on him, ever so slowly.

Nutty took a step back, and then another. But he had no idea which direction he was going. Was he out on the stage? Could he step off into some orchestra pit or down some trapdoor? Maybe that's what William had done. But that would have made a noise, and Nutty had heard absolutely nothing. No footsteps, no slumping to the floor. Nothing.

And still the breathing was there. Definitely closer.

Nutty stepped back again and bumped into

something soft but solid. He jumped ahead, and then spun around. "William, is that you?"

But now the breathing was behind him again, and he spun back the other way. "Don't. Please. William, if that's you, tell me."

Something was there, close enough to touch, and yet the sound was behind Nutty too. All around him. The panic was welling up, and Nutty would have run if he had known which direction to go. "Don't. Please don't. Don't hurt me," he blurted out. But the sound of his own voice echoed around the room and was almost as scary as the silence, the breathing.

"I just want to talk to you, Mr. Graham," Nutty whispered. "I don't like the movie either."

And then that strange, vague glow—the one he had seen in his room—began to form before him, not more than five or six feet away. Nutty stepped back again and felt his back strike something solid, maybe a wall. Nutty wasn't about to go forward again. He was locked in place.

The glow was taking on a distinctive shape, the way it had in his room. Nutty was beginning to see the skinny frame, the long legs.

"Really. I just want to talk to you," Nutty said again. "I only want to—" But his voice cracked and then stopped.

And then the ghost spoke, low and mellow, "I warned you. You didn't keep your promise."

114

"Okay. I know. But I will now. I don't want to finish the movie. I know how bad it is."

"Depart from this place. Never go back to the movie set."

"Okay. Okay. That's a deal. But I don't know which way to go."

Instantly a little backstage light came on, and Nutty could see enough to know where he was. He was leaning against the back of a big over-stuffed chair, apparently part of some set. But he knew which direction the door was now, and he could get away. The figure was still before him, but it was less clear in the half-light.

Nutty slipped sideways, and then started to back away toward the door. The figure didn't move, but Nutty wanted to keep his eyes on it.

He was almost to the door when he realized he couldn't do this. What about William? He couldn't just cut and run, and leave William. "Excuse me," Nutty said, with great effort, "but do you know where my friend William is?"

"Depart this place," the voice said, and it moved toward him, not walking, but floating, it seemed.

Nutty backed to the door and put one hand on the doorknob, but he didn't leave. "I can't leave without William. Did you hurt him?"

"Depart." The thing stopped, but it was easier to see now, and the face looked full of rage.

"Uh . . . I don't think I ought to do that. If you could just send him out, we'll both go."

Again the shape moved forward, and now, in a booming, echoing voice, it said, "Depart! Now!"

Nutty turned the doorknob and pulled the door open. But he didn't leave. "Look, I can't leave without him. I'm afraid he's hurt or something. You don't have any right to hurt people. I don't care what Deveraux did to you. You shouldn't be knocking guys around and stuff like that."

Nutty opened the door all the way and prepared to run if the figure made a grab for him.

But a long pause followed. The ghost stood his ground. Nutty's breath seemed trapped in his chest, and his head was buzzing with the terror that was quivering through his whole body. But he didn't leave.

And then Nutty heard the last thing he expected. The guy started to laugh.

Suddenly the figure lost its glow and turned into an ordinary looking man—except for the strange clothes.

And he kept right on laughing. It wasn't one of those ghost story laughs, all full of hoots and howls. The guy just sort of chuckled to himself, like a person who had thought of something funny. And then he said, "You're some kid, you know that? You've got some grit in you. I gave you my best spook bit, and you stood right up to me."

116

Nutty was stunned. He had no idea what to do now. Finally he thought to say, "Could you get William for me now?"

And Mr. Graham said, chuckling again, "I thought you wanted to talk to me." He was actually sounding very easygoing, and quite American. The British accent was gone.

"I do. But I'm worried about William."

"All right. All right. You strike a hard bargain, kid."

Another few seconds passed in silence, and then Nutty heard William say, "Nutty. Nutty. What's happening?" He staggered out of the darkness toward the door.

The ghost answered for Nutty. "Well, I let you take a little nap, that's all."

William threw himself against the wall, next to Nutty. "Who said that?" he whispered, and his voice seemed to catch in his throat.

Nutty pointed to Mr. Graham, who was still standing in the shadows. "I tried to run you two off," Mr. Graham said. "But your old buddy—Nutty, as you call him—wouldn't leave without you. He's some pal, I'll tell you."

William seemed to find courage in hearing the casual way the ghost was speaking. "We came to find you, sir. We want to talk to you."

"Yeah, yeah. I know. Well, all right. I guess you've earned that much."

He stepped out of the shadows, and he didn't seem ghostly at all.

William reached out his hand and said, "Nice to meet you, sir."

The man laughed. "Sorry, I don't do handshakes."

"Are you dead?" William asked.

"Well, that depends on how you look at it, I suppose. But let's not talk about that. What do you want from me?"

"We think you're trying to stop the movie," William said, "but we don't want anyone to get hurt."

"Look, I don't either," Mr. Graham said. "And I'll admit, I tossed that actor a little too far, but it's hard to know your own strength sometimes. I have a lot of power I didn't have back when . . . well, before. But I'm not backing off. I'm stopping that movie, no matter what."

"Hey, I want out," Nutty said. "It's the worst movie ever made."

This really cracked up Mr. Graham. "Son, I like you," he said. "Let's go to the greenroom. We can sit down and talk this thing over."

And so off they went, as though this sort of thing happened every day. Nutty found himself thinking that the guy couldn't possibly be a ghost. But how else could he do all that stuff?

118

In the greenroom, backstage—the place where actors relax while they're waiting to go on stage—were some nice soft chairs. Mr. Graham invited the boys to sit down, and he sat across from them. He cocked one long leg up with his ankle across his knee, and he said, "Okay, here's the deal. I'm not stopping until this movie is dead. You might as well know that right now."

"Why?" William asked.

"Look, young man, I don't answer questions. I'll tell you what I want to tell you. Is that understood?"

"Well, sure. But I was just sort of curious."

"Hey, I know all about your curiosity. But if you think you're going to get me on tape, or get a picture of me, forget it. Don't you think I knew you were under that bed? You made more noise than a kid with a toy drum."

Nutty suddenly realized why he had heard noises that night.

"I'm not trying to get proof of anything anymore, sir, but I can't help but wonder how you—"

"Fine. You just keep wondering. All I agreed to do was talk. And our only subject is the movie."

"That's okay with us," Nutty said. "I hate doing it. I know I'm not a good actor."

Mr. Graham chuckled again. "Hey, I'm glad

you said it, so I didn't have to. I mean, you really stink."

Nutty shrugged. It wasn't the word he would have chosen, but the point was still the same.

"Here's our problem," William said. "I agree, Nutty is pathetic as an actor."

William's choice of words was a little more annoying, but Nutty still let it go.

"He wants out of the movie. But Deveraux is threatening him with law suits and jail and everything else. By the way, did you appear as Nutty and do the vandalism?"

Mr. Graham looked rather shamefaced. "Well, yeah. That was kind of a cheap trick, I guess. But Deveraux is lying. I didn't really damage anything of any value. And by the way, that's the last question I answer. You're a tricky little guy, you know that? Are you really a kid? You talk like a great-uncle of mine."

"Sorry, sir, but I don't feel that I have to answer your questions either," William said, and he and the ghost had a very good laugh.

Nutty couldn't believe this was happening.

"But you see the problem," William said. "The police have an eyewitness, and Deveraux can press charges. Besides that, Nutty is under contract. If he drops out of the movie, Deveraux can sue him."

"Sure. I see the problem." Mr. Graham uncrossed his legs and leaned forward. He seemed to think things over. "I guess I've tried to be a little too subtle," he finally said. "The whole idea was to haunt the movie, make Deveraux nervous and scare him out—without being too obvious. But that didn't work. Besides, I was so sick of old Parker's acting by then, I thought I'd run him off and maybe do a little service to the profession in the bargain. But I guess now it's time to take the bull by the horns. I've got to put a real scare into Deveraux. Maybe you fellows can help me."

"Sure. No problem," William said, and he sounded rather excited by the idea. "What if you appeared at the—"

"Wait a minute!" Nutty said. "William, you don't make the deals."

William nodded. "Okay. You're right." He sat back. "You two talk."

"I don't want any injuries—not to anyone," Nutty said.

"I don't either," Mr. Graham said. "I'm just thinking of taking on old Deveraux directly. He'll be terrified if he sees me. He knows I'm . . . not around anymore."

"But if you scare Mr. Deveraux away, won't the movie company lose a lot of money?"

"Deveraux himself put up all the money for this one. And he's loaded, big-time. He made enough off a stinkeroo of a movie that I did for him to pay for the losses on this one ten times over. So I don't figure I owe him anything. What I want is for him to leave movie-making all together."

"I thought the movie you did got awful reviews."

"Sure it did. Do you think that matters at the box office? People love this junk the guy turns out. If he finishes this thing, you'll be a superstar, Parker. Every movie company in the country will be after you."

"Oh, brother, we gotta stop it," Nutty said. "But what about all the actors? Wouldn't they lose the money they were going to make?"

"I'll tell you, kid, you consider all the fine points. I tend not to worry about those things much anymore."

William jumped on that one. "You mean, sir, that once you're dead, you—"

"No way, Willie, my boy. I'm not telling you one more thing. We're not supposed to tell any of this stuff. We've got rules. I'm probably in trouble already."

"But what about the actors?" Nutty asked again. He wanted to settle the deal and move on. This whole thing was still pretty eerie.

"Okay. Let's see. Maybe I can scare him into paying off. How would that be?"

Nutty nodded. "That's good," he said. "Why didn't you just do that in the first place?"

"Hey, come on. It's not like I've got a lot of experience at this haunting shtick. I'm sort of working it out as I go along."

Nutty nodded. "Okay," he said. But then he asked, "So what do we do now?"

"Just go back to the set and say you're sorry you walked off. You'll finish the film. I'll take it from there."

Nutty thought for a few seconds. He had a lot of questions, but he decided to trust the guy. "Well, okay," he said.

"Look, before we end this," William said, "could I just ask one little question about the way things—"

"Forget it, kid," Mr. Graham said.

And—*zap*—he disappeared.

Chapter 11

"Oh, Parker, I love you. I forgive you. I'll never doubt you again."

Mr. Deveraux, needless to say, was thrilled that Nutty had decided to return the next day. And he was soon setting up to do the fight scene all over again.

"We've got to rush," he kept saying. "We're very far behind schedule."

Nutty didn't say much. Mostly he just waited to see what would happen.

And it didn't take long.

The men practiced the fight scene one more time, and Nutty wiped them out with all his amazing skills. But on the first take, Deveraux shouted, "Action," and Nutty stepped forward to face his attacker. He flipped the guy over and turned to face the second man. Suddenly, next to Nutty appeared . . . another Nutty.

Nutty glanced, and then did a double take. For a moment he thought someone had moved a mirror next to him. The figure was dressed the same. He *was* the same. The same overalls, the same body, same face. Maybe the eyes looked a little strange.

But the figure said, "Together, good friend, we can be victorious. Let's have at them, shall be?" And then Nutty heard that chuckle. It was Graham's voice, Graham's laugh, not Nutty's.

But the Hell's Cherubs didn't charge. The fight suddenly ended, and everyone on the set seemed frozen. Nutty looked over at Deveraux. The man's body had turned to stone. His eyes were locked on the two "Parkers," but nothing came from his lips.

"Oh, Damian, I'm sorry," Mr. Graham said. "I didn't mean to startle you. I just thought the scene would be more believable with two guys doing the fighting. I mean, really, do you expect the audience to buy the idea that one skinny farm kid can fight a whole gang?"

Not a move from Deveraux. Not even a blink.

"Excuse me," the figure said. "I'm sorry. I've really shocked you. I guess you don't recognize me in this form. It's Matthew Graham. Remember me?"

He reached out a hand.

Nutty took a quick look around. People were

trying to deal with their confusion. They were glancing around at each other, but otherwise, they were hardly moving.

Deveraux mumbled something Nutty couldn't understand and shrank back from the outstretched hand.

"Don't worry," the ghost said. "You think you're seeing double, or hallucinating, or some such thing. When actually, I'm an old acquaintance, returned from . . . *the grave.* Since you ruined the last part of my life, it seemed only fair that I return the favor."

"Enemies," Deveraux whispered, and he seemed to be finding some strength. "I have so many enemies."

And in that instant Nutty Number Two turned into Mr. Graham, in his Shakespearean dress. "Not *enemies*, Damian. Just an old friend."

"Graham," Deveraux said, "you're not dead. It's all tricks. Special effects. You want me to go crazy. But I won't do it."

"No, no, Damian, you have the wrong idea entirely. All I want you to do is shut down this film and get out of town. Please do."

"Parker put you up to this. And that boy-man— *Bilks.* You're all out to make me crazy."

"Well, maybe. I suppose that's possible." Graham put his hand to his chin and pretended to think. By now, people around the set were backing away. Nutty saw his spectator friends all clinging together but not making a sound. "But I'm sure you're a very sane man. You won't mind if I hang around you from now on—in your hotel rooms, in your limousine. Hey, I'll even go home with you, and just hover around your house night and day. Maybe I could suddenly appear from time to time—just to wake you up in the middle of the night or to entertain your guests."

The momentary confidence left Deveraux's face as the possibility that Graham was a ghost really took hold. After a few seconds of silence, he began to panic.

"Why? Why? Why are you doing this, Graham? I paid you well."

"Yes, that's true. But you shamed me. I can't seem to get comfortable in—well, you know, where I am. All I can think of all day long is that I shamed myself in your awful movie. So I took a long look around and found you were making another film—one that was even worse, if that's possible. I just *couldn't* let you do that."

"Leave me alone. Go away."

"I can't do that, Damian. Not until you make me some promises."

"What? What?" Deveraux was sweating profusely.

"I want you to stop this movie and leave this town. And I want you to—how shall I say it? I want you to retire. I want you to live on what you have—live very nicely—but never make another movie. Will you do that, Damian—for me?"

"I can't do that!" Deveraux moaned.

"Well, fine. You have a nice place. I don't mind living there and making your life far more miserable than I have here."

"All right. All right. I'll do it. I'll quit making movies."

Nutty glanced around. He was wondering how people would react. But actually, they all looked like statues—all staring, not believing their own eyes.

"Now, Damian," Graham said, "you have a bad reputation for breaking promises. If you break this one, remember: *I'll . . . be . . . baaaaa-aaaack.*"

"All right. All right. Just leave."

"You leave first."

"All right. I'll do that."

Finally Nutty got up the nerve to yell, "Mr. Graham, remember the actors."

"Oh, yes, excuse me," Graham said. "One other matter. Everyone gets paid for this film. Believe me, they earned their money."

"All right. Whatever you say."

"Well, then, get going." And suddenly Graham jumped at Deveraux.

128

Deveraux took off like a shot. He ran straight to his limousine. "Get me out of here," he yelled to the driver, and he jumped in the backseat. Then he spun around and shouted out the window, "This movie is history. It's in the toilet. I won't ever come back to this stupid place again as long as I live. I'm going where my enemies will never find me again!"

And away the limousine sped.

Nutty couldn't believe the good news. He looked back to thank Mr. Graham.

But he was gone.

It was a very strange moment. People were all looking at Nutty now, seeming to have realized that he knew more about this than they did. Nutty shrugged his shoulders and said, "Hey, let's just be happy this whole thing is over."

But no one moved.

Only William found the voice to say, "Cut!"

Nutty realized that the camera had been going the whole time.

William hurried to the cameraman and said, "Let's get the film to the developer. It could be very interesting material."

Nutty laughed a little and looked around. Sarah was still locked in shock. Her eyes were wide open, and they were trained on Nutty.

"It's kind of hard to explain," Nutty said.

He shrugged.

And she laughed.

*   *   *

The next several days were very strange. The newspaper ran an odd story about the movie coming to a close. The reporter printed lots of eerie details from the accounts she got from the actors and other observers. But the versions varied wildly, as everyone tried to account, somehow, for what they had seen. It all sounded like special effects gone crazy, or the overly imaginative visions of a bunch of crazy actors.

Rumors spread around town, and the story changed every time. The kids who had been there, just watching, told their parents that a ghost had appeared, but a day or two later their parents had convinced them that they hadn't really seen what they had seen. One common theory was that some Hollywood type had used lasers to create the image everyone had seen.

And so the ghost story didn't hold up very well. After all, everyone knew that ghosts don't exist.

William was probably the most disappointed. He showed up at Nutty's house on the second morning after the sudden end of the movie. He found Nutty sleeping in, and he scared him half to death by coming into his room and tapping on his shoulder.

But once Nutty was conscious and could

breathe normally, without gasping, William said, "Bad news. Graham's not on the film. You can hear what Deveraux says, but none of the rest. People who watch it without seeing what we saw will just think Deveraux cracked up and was seeing things that weren't there."

"William, that's good. I don't want to believe in all that stuff anyway. I don't want to be that scared again, not ever."

"How can you *not* believe it?"

"I don't know. Can't we do one of those *Wizard of Oz* endings, and just sort of say the whole thing was a bad dream?"

"Well, we could, but how would you explain what happened to your summer?"

"Maybe it was a long bad dream."

"And what about all the money in your bank account?"

"Uh . . . I sleepwalk. I rob banks."

"I don't know. I hope you don't get caught."

Nutty laughed. "I guess I also couldn't explain about my dad being so mad."

"Yeah, what's he saying about all this?"

"He thinks everyone has gone crazy. He doesn't believe any of it. He still thinks I can get in some other movies, though. He wants me to keep acting."

William chuckled to hear that, and then he sat

down next to Nutty on his bed. "What did you tell him?"

"Well, he doesn't want to listen, but I've told him that I won't do something I'm not good at—and that I don't want to do."

"Well, at least you got yourself a nice piece of cash out of the deal."

"That's what I told Dad. Now I can go to college whenever I want, and I'll figure out what I want to do with myself."

"That sounds pretty grown-up, Nutty. Maybe this whole thing was good for you."

Nutty shook his head. "It wasn't worth it to me. Was it to you?"

"Well, it was interesting. I just wish that I could prove the whole thing one way or the other. I sort of agree with you. I think maybe it didn't happen the way it—you know—the way it appeared to happen."

"What are you talking about? You saw everything."

"Sort of. But I'm a scientist, Nutty. If I go around telling this story, people are going to lose all trust in me. Besides, I found something out that makes me wonder."

Nutty sat up. This was unbelievable. "Are you saying that Graham wasn't really a ghost?"

"No. Not necessarily. But I found out that he

started his career as a magician, and he dabbled in that kind of stuff all his life."

"How could he glow in the dark and change forms and everything? How could he show up as *me?*"

"I don't know. But I don't know how magicians cut people in half either. Maybe it was all a bunch of tricks."

"Graham died two years ago. You know that."

"Yeah. But there's been some talk about that too. He once appeared in a play where a guy faked his own death, collected the insurance, and lived very well from then on. Maybe that's what he did. He was very bitter against Deveraux. Maybe he was a con man and just set this whole thing up to get rid of the guy."

"No way. You know better than that, William."

"Well, I don't know." William got up and walked across the room. He turned Nutty's desk chair around and sat down on it. "Let's just say, I'd rather believe the world can be explained. I don't like loose ends."

"Sure. No one does. But we know what we saw."

"Yes. But believing what you *think* you see is very tricky, Nutty. I'd rather keep the whole thing on hold for now and not say much more about it. I don't want to get a reputation for being a flake."

"Hey, I'm with you on that one," Nutty said. He sat up and threw his feet over the side of the bed. "I'd rather just forget it."

"Good. Let's do that. Let's just tell people we think the whole thing can be explained in . . . natural ways."

"Okay. I even think maybe it could be. Somehow."

Nutty and William both liked that.

They decided not to talk about it anymore. Nutty got up and got dressed, and the two of them found something to eat. After that, they walked over to Sarah's, just to see what she was doing.

Sarah was still very confused by everything she had seen. But she told Nutty and William she didn't believe in ghosts. She thought maybe she had been out in the sun too long that day.

Sure, that made sense.

In fact, William and Nutty told her they thought it was a very good explanation.

They dropped the whole subject.

After a while, Orlando stopped by. He had a new pair of shades. He thought maybe those last ones messed up his vision.

That made sense too.

It was amazing how many things were making sense all of a sudden. Nutty was glad to spend his time with such wise, clear-thinking friends.

"The thing is," Orlando said. "I don't believe in ghosts."

"I don't either," Sarah said.

"Hey, I'm with you guys," Nutty said.

And William added, "Scientifically speaking, ghosts seem highly unlikely."

And so they all agreed, and Nutty said, "Let's just try to forget the whole thing."

But just then a low chuckle sounded somewhere not far away—the sound of a guy laughing to himself. It was followed by an eerie whispering sound, and Nutty thought he heard the words: "You're forgetting. I'm the one who warned you."

Everyone stopped. Nutty saw the blood drain from Sarah's face. He suddenly felt a little lightheaded himself.

"Did you hear that?" Orlando said.

There was a long pause before William said, "Hear what?"

And then Sarah said, "I didn't hear anything. Did you hear anything, Nutty?"

Nutty thought it over. "I don't think so. I *thought* I did, but now I . . . I don't think I did after all."

"Right," Orlando said. "That's how it was for me too."

And William said, "In fact, I don't even think that I *thought* I heard anything."

Everyone agreed. Now that they thought about it a little more, no one thought that they had thought that they had heard anything before they decided they hadn't.

Now things were really making sense.

Except that Nutty had a notion that he could still hear something—that same chuckling sound, moving steadily away.

But no. It couldn't be. Everything can be explained.